GUNS, WIVES
AND
CHOCOLATE

Sally Berneathy

Books by Sally Berneathy

Death by Chocolate
(book 1 in the Death by Chocolate series)

Murder, Lies and Chocolate
(book 2 in the Death by Chocolate series)

The Great Chocolate Scam
(book 3 in the Death by Chocolate series)

Chocolate Mousse Attack
(book 4 in the Death by Chocolate series)

Fatal Chocolate Obsession
(book 5 in the Death by Chocolate series)

Deadly Chocolate Addiction
(book 6 in the Death by Chocolate series)

Guns, Wives and Chocolate
(book 7 in the Death by Chocolate series)

The Ex Who Wouldn't Die
(book 1 in Charley's Ghost series)

The Ex Who Glowed in the Dark
(book 2 in Charley's Ghost series)

The Ex Who Conned a Psychic
(book 3 in Charley's Ghost series)

The Ex Who Saw a Ghost
(book 4 in Charley's Ghost series)

The Ex Who Hid a Deadly Past
(book 5 in Charley's Ghost series)

This book is a work of fiction. The names, characters, places and incidents are products of the writer's imagination or have been used fictitiously and are not to be construed as real. Any resemblance to persons, living or dead, or to actual events, locales or organizations is entirely coincidental (except for Fred and King Henry).

Guns, Wives and Chocolate
Copyright ©2018 Sally Berneathy

This book may not be reproduced in whole or in part without written permission from
Sally Berneathy.
http://www.sallyberneathy.com

Original cover art by Cheryl Welch
http://www.mywelchdesign.com/

Chapter One

A welcome home party to celebrate a drug dealer's release from prison.

What could possibly go wrong with that?

Harold and Cathy Murray, grandparents of that drug dealer, arrived at my house on Saturday afternoon.

"Come in," I invited. "Good to see you!" It was true. I liked the elderly couple who'd once owned my house.

Their grandson, George, the party honoree...not so much.

He was nowhere in sight. Maybe he wouldn't show up for his own party.

"Isn't this a beautiful day?" Cathy's pink cheeks glowed, and her white curls bounced. "The sun is out, the redbuds and forsythia are already blooming. I think this early spring is a good sign for George."

The early spring might be due to global warming or a groundhog who didn't see his shadow last month, but I was pretty sure it had nothing to do with George. If a tornado loomed on the horizon, I could give him credit for that, but a bright spring day? No.

Harold, carrying two grocery bags, came in behind his wife. "Meat, buns, and chips." His lips smiled but his eyes didn't. "George is having a cigarette before he brings the potato salad in."

Note to self: *Don't eat the potato salad.*

"Everything's ready out back," I said. "Trent's got the fire going, chocolate chip cookies are on the patio table, and the ice chests are loaded with Cokes and bottled water."

The Murrays had specified no alcoholic beverages since they thought George might have addiction issues.

Years of using drugs, six years in prison for selling drugs...*you think?*

I looked out to the street where George leaned against the Murrays' white sedan. He blew a stream of smoke in my direction.

I'd agreed to this welcome home party over two years ago because the Murrays were such sweet people. Who knew George would actually get out of prison?

But he did.

The future was now.

He tossed his cigarette to the ground and crushed it with his heel, all the time focusing his angry gaze on me as if he knew I was thinking about him.

A moving truck rumbled down the street, diverting his attention before he could incinerate me with his stare.

My new neighbors?

The eighty-nine year old widower who'd lived across the street and down one house had moved to

Arizona to marry the younger woman he'd met online, a woman in her seventies. He was such a cradle robber.

My ex, Rickhead, immediately snatched up the property as an investment. These must be the new tenants.

Much as I wanted to find out more about them, I had to play hostess rather than nosy neighbor. There'd be time for that later.

I closed the door and went through the house to the back yard.

Smoke trailed lazily upward up from the grill on one side of the patio. A tall, good-looking guy in faded jeans and a red T-shirt with the logo of the local football team stood beside the grill. He wielded a spatula in one hand and held his other out to shake with Harold.

The sight of that tall, good-looking guy brought the happy to my heart. I would enjoy this party in spite of George as long as Trent—Detective Adam Trent—was with me. He had tried to talk me out of doing this but, when that failed, he'd settled for being here to keep an eye on everything. I could handle George, but I was glad for any excuse to have Trent around.

Harold put his bags on the patio table and accepted Trent's hand. "Really appreciate you all doing this."

Cathy set a tray of condiments beside my platter of cookies and gave Trent a hug. "Knowing he's accepted will help George get back into a normal life."

How could he get back into something he'd never had?

Cathy turned to the other side of the patio. "Fred, Sophie, so glad you all could make it."

Fred and Sophie? Together? Drat! I hadn't seen them arrive.

Fred lives next door, so he would have come from his back yard to mine, but Sophie lives across the street. She must have been at Fred's house already. For how long? All night? I knew…suspected…they were having a relationship and it made me crazy that they wouldn't tell me. They frustrated my nosy gene.

The two of them lounged in matching folding chairs and held matching crystal glasses. I felt certain those glasses did not contain a soft drink.

Cathy hugged them both. "You look gorgeous, Sophie."

She always did. Long, dark, straight hair, olive skin, and a beautiful smile.

"Lindsay, do you need some help?" Sophie offered.

"Thanks, but everything's ready."

George came skulking around the side of the house.

I stopped.

He stopped.

Cathy hurried over and took the large plastic bowl from him. "George, sweetheart, come meet everybody."

He draped an arm around her shoulders and his gaze softened. Maybe he wasn't one hundred percent bad if he loved his grandmother. "Nana, I invited a friend. Is that okay?"

Her smile remained in place but appeared a little forced. "Of course it's okay. After all, this is your party."

"Thanks! This is Gaylord Dumford."

4

A sinister version of the Howdy Doody puppet from the '50s children's show slouched into view behind George. "Brought the birthday boy a present." Howdy Doody held up a large bottle of bourbon.

He hadn't heard about Cathy's no-alcohol request.

Or didn't care.

Cathy ignored the booze and introduced her grandson and his buddy around the group as if this were tea at the country club and Gaylord Dumford was George's best friend from high school.

More likely his former cellmate.

From across the patio came a sizzling sound followed by a mouth-watering aroma.

"How does everybody like their burgers cooked?" Trent asked.

"Medium," I replied.

"Burnt," Harold said.

"Medium." Fred gave his glass to Sophie and stood. "I'll get more chairs."

By the time he returned with four chairs, we needed more.

George had a lot of friends.

Some of them brought beer.

Somebody passed around bourbon in paper cups.

They laughed and talked and drank.

Cathy, Harold, and I huddled over by the grill with Trent.

The warm spring day had developed a chill in spite of the bright sunshine.

"I'm so sorry," Cathy said. "He didn't tell me he was going to invite his friends."

Harold frowned. "I didn't know he had any friends."

"It's okay," I said. "No problem." Those damn manners my mother forced on me. It was not even close to *okay*.

"Lindsay!"

I turned toward the sound of my name and froze.

The woman coming around the house could not be…

Her bright red hair glowed in the dying rays of the sun and her bright red lips smiled widely.

Grace. Rickhead's first ex.

"I saw all the cars and thought you must be having a party," she said. "I know you won't mind if Rickie stays here for a little while until we get everything moved into the house. He has so much energy, he keeps getting in the way of the movers, and we don't want one of them to trip."

"You're moving?" *Please don't let this be related to that van I saw!*

"Didn't Rick tell you? He bought the house across from Paula, and Chuck and I are renting it. We're going to be neighbors!"

"Neighbors?" I'd have chosen a serial killer who kept bodies in the basement over Grace and Rickie for my new neighbors!

Rickie sidled up. "I've missed you, Aunt Lindsay." Rickhead's eleven year old son has his mother's big brown eyes and his father's gift for being a con artist.

"It'll be easier for Chuck to find a job here than in Crappie Creek," Grace said. "He travels so much, he's hardly ever home with his family." She beamed up at the skinny bearded man behind her.

Chuck. Her new husband.

My new neighbors.

Gaylord sauntered over to join us. The phony grin that spread across his broad face made him look even more like a psychotic Howdy Doody. "Hey, Chuckie!"

Grace's husband knew one of George's friends? Not a good sign.

Chuck stiffened. "Hey. How you doing, Dumford?"

"Got something here you're gonna like." Howdy extended a homemade cigarette.

Chuck lifted his hand, and for a moment I thought he was going to accept.

Instead he took a package of gum from his shirt pocket and unwrapped a stick. "Thanks. I quit." He put the gum in his mouth and chewed.

"Chuck quit smoking for Rickie and me." Grace beamed up at her husband.

He beamed down at her.

I was pretty sure the item offered was not a nicotine type cigarette, but Chuck didn't smoke whatever it was anymore, and Grace was happy.

"Honey," Grace said, "would you grab Rickie before he drinks that beer?"

I wasn't *honey*, but I dashed to the table where Rickie was lifting a can to his mouth.

I snatched it from him.

He glared at me.

"Don't you think you're a little young for that, especially with a cop standing a few feet away?"

"My daddy lets me drink beer."

"I do not."

Interesting. Chuck acknowledged the *daddy* reference. Chuck climbed a notch in my book.

Rickie sneered. "My real daddy."

"No, he doesn't." I wouldn't have put such a thing past my ex, but I knew he'd never spent enough time with his son for them to have a beer together.

"Rickie, Chuck is your daddy now." Grace wrapped an arm around her husband. "He's adopting Rickie and then we'll be a real family. Rick signed the papers and we accepted five years free rent on the house for back child support. We go before the judge on Monday to make it official."

I wasn't even a little surprised that Rickhead would so easily give up custody of his son.

My regard for Chuck went up another notch. If he was willing to take on the job of parenting this demon child, he had my respect.

"Can I have a cookie?" the demon child asked.

The fact that he'd asked instead of grabbing one told me Chuck was teaching him some manners.

"Of course you can. Grace, Chuck, help yourselves to cookies. When you finish unpacking for the day, you'll be too tired to cook, so please come over and grab a burger." I started to say we'd have a lot of food left over, but I wasn't sure that would be true with such a large gathering of George's friends. "I'll save some for you."

"Thank you!" Grace gushed. She took a cookie and handed one to Chuck. "Lindsay makes the best cookies in the world."

I couldn't disagree.

Rickie munched on his cookie as he pushed through the noisy crowd toward the grill where Trent was moving cooked meat patties to a platter. "Can I have a hamburger?"

"You bet." Trent's a sucker for kids, even demon spawn kids. "Grab a plate and a bun."

"Rickie wants to be a policeman like Trent when he grows up," Grace said.

I ignored her fanciful comment. Let her keep her dreams about her miscreant son for a few more years. "You should probably take Rickie home with you. I'm not sure you want him to be around these people."

"He'll be fine. We're not worried with Trent and Fred here." She waved in Fred's direction.

Fred took a long drink of whatever was in his glass.

"The pretty lady with him must be Sophie," Grace said. "Rickie told me all about her. He adores her."

And Sophie adored him. She's even more delusional about kids than Cathy and Trent.

Smoke came from another source besides the grill.

"You can't smoke out here!" I pushed my way to the man with a cigarette in his hand. "Take it to the street!"

The big bearded man looked at me and took another puff.

I yanked the cigarette out of his mouth and stomped on it.

His gross features burst into a creditable imitation of Wolfman. He grabbed my shoulders with two big paws.

"Is there a problem?" Trent's voice came from behind me.

The talk and laughter stopped. Cops have that effect on criminals.

Wolfman took his paws off my shoulders and looked sheepish.

"I'll show you the way to the street." Trent's voice was quiet and deadly.

Wolfman flinched. "No, man, it's all good. Didn't see the no smoking sign."

"Didn't post one," I said. "Didn't know you could read."

Wolfman gave me the evil eye, gulped from his paper cup, and turned his back to us.

Trent returned to the grill, and I looked around for Grace. She and Chuck were leaving, already halfway around the house. Rickie stood at the table, adding mustard and onions to his burger.

I started after Grace and Chuck.

Howdy Doody was ahead of me. He grabbed Chuck's arm.

Were they going to have a fight? Could this party get any worse?

Loud, raucous music burst through the evening air.

Yes.

I stomped through the crowd toward a short, skinny guy with a paper cup of something in one hand and a cell phone in the other. The loud noise came from the phone. I snatched it from him.

"Hey!" he protested. "That's mine!"

I switched it off. "You turn it on again, and it's mine. I'll give it to the cop over there at the grill and let him run the serial number to find out if it's stolen."

His eyes popped as he looked in Trent's direction.

I dropped the phone into his lap.

Another man took his cigarette from his mouth and crushed it on the pavement, his gaze never leaving mine. I could almost read his thoughts. *Red-headed bitch is crazy. I better humor her.*

A wise decision.

What was I doing before the latest interruption? Oh, yeah, trying to catch Grace and Chuck so I could return Rickie to them.

Grace and Chuck were gone. Rickie was not. That was not a good thing.

Howdy Doody was also gone and there was no blood on the ground. That was a good thing.

Rickie had settled into a chair between two of George's friends. All three munched on burgers.

Music exploded from the crowd.

I started in that direction but Fred beat me to it.

Just as well because another man was lighting up a cigarette over by Trent.

My personal cop spoke a few words in his ear. The man paled and dropped the cigarette.

"Rickie," I said, "Sophie would like for you to join her." I turned in her direction. "Wouldn't you, Sophie?"

She smiled and waved.

Rickie returned her wave. "Nah, I want to stay here with my new homies. They got lots of funny stories."

I gritted my teeth. *He's just a child*, I reminded myself. Sometimes he and I got along okay. Sometimes I kind of liked him. This wasn't one of those times. "Rickie, if you don't get up, take your chair, and join Sophie right now, I'm going to have Trent put you in handcuffs and drag you over there."

"Cool!"

I grabbed his ear. I'd seen his grandmother use that technique on his grown uncles.

"Ow!" he shrieked. "You hurt me! I'm gonna call social services."

"Go ahead! What are they going to do? Tell me I can't get within a hundred feet of you? Gosh, that would break my heart!"

A hand touched my shoulder.

I spun around, ready to hit somebody.

It was Fred. I didn't hit him. "Maybe you should go inside, have a brownie and relax. I'll take care of this."

I opened my mouth to protest then closed it. Fred was right. I was losing it. I needed to calm down, let Fred handle Rickie.

I pushed through the obnoxious guests and made my way to Trent.

He studied me closely as I approached. "You okay?"

"Not really. I'm going inside for a few minutes."

"Good idea." He flipped another burger and scanned the crowd. "Fred and I can control your guests."

"Invaders, you mean. When this is over, I'm going to kill George."

12

Cathy appeared at my side. "You'll have to get in line behind Harold and me."

Cathy was ready to kill her grandson? I wasn't overreacting. Things were as bad as they seemed.

"Want to come inside with me?" I asked. "I have a box of wine in the refrigerator."

Cathy's lips settled into a grim line. "Thank you, but we're trying to find George and get him to send his friends home. The last time I saw him, he had a beer in one hand and a cigarette in the other. I'm so sorry this happened. George never mentioned inviting all these people. I'm sure he didn't know they'd behave so badly."

She was the perennial optimist.

"We'll find him and take care of this." Harold stood behind his wife. His expression went beyond grim, all the way to furious.

I liked the Murrays. I wanted to reassure them that everything was fine, all the uninvited guests were no problem.

Even in the interest of good manners, I couldn't tell a lie that big.

I went inside.

King Henry, the cat who moved in and took over a couple of years ago, looked up from his position beside the basement door. His sky blue eyes were stormy. He returned his gaze to the door and switched his tail across the kitchen floor.

His actions brought back unpleasant memories of the time people kept breaking into my house and digging up my basement, looking for drug money George had buried when his grandparents lived there.

Henry snarled and pawed at the bottom of the door.

Suddenly everything made sense.

George's insistence that we have his party at my house rather than his grandparents'.

The people George invited to his party.

The way those people kept causing problems...playing music, smoking, drinking...things to divert my attention.

It wasn't because he had such fond memories of visiting his grandparents when they lived here. It was because George thought the money was still buried in my basement.

I grabbed my marble rolling pin off the counter.

I would be first in line to kill George after all.

I flung open the door. The light at the bottom of the stairs was on. No surprise.

Henry darted down the steps ahead of me.

My cat weighs twenty-three pounds, all muscle. With his half-inch claws and teeth, he could take George down before I got there. I didn't want that to happen. I wanted to be part of the takedown.

I hefted the rolling pin over my shoulder and charged down the stairs. Henry was a few feet ahead of me as we crossed through the basement to the old furnace room where coal had been delivered when my house and the twentieth century were young.

Henry stopped at the open door, tail in the air, hair on the back of his neck standing straight up, waiting for me so we could attack together. We're a team.

In the corner of the small, dark room, George was so intent on digging up the floor he didn't see either of us.

Fred and I had worked hard to get the bricks in that area smooth. He'd even used a level. When I got through with George, Fred was going to kill him too.

"Hey!" I shouted.

George looked up, startled.

"The money's long gone, and you're going to put every brick back in place, then you're going to go upstairs and send your horrible friends home!"

He raised his shovel threateningly.

Hadn't counted on that. Shovel trumps rolling pin.

Henry hissed.

I reached down and put my hand on his head. Sometimes Henry over-estimates his own abilities. I wasn't sure he realized that shovel trumps half inch claws and teeth.

Henry stilled but remained tense, ready to spring.

"What did you do with my money?" George demanded.

"Tiger Lily probably found it," I said, referring to his girlfriend he'd sent to retrieve it while he was in prison. She was in prison now so she was safe even if he believed me.

"You're lying."

It wasn't exactly a lie. I'd said *probably*.

"Lindsay, are you down there?" Trent called.

On one hand, I was irritated he'd followed me. But on the other hand, the most important hand, gun trumps shovel.

"Arrest this man! He broke into my home and is digging in my basement!"

George lowered his shovel. "I didn't break in. I was invited to a party. I have every right to be here."

15

"Why were you digging up her basement?" Trent knew why. He didn't know what had happened to the money, but he knew George had put it there.

George threw down the shovel and started for the door. "I gotta get back to my grandma. She's gonna be worried about me."

I blocked his exit. He no longer had a shovel. I had a rolling pin, a cat, and a cop. I was suddenly brave. "Not until you put that floor back the way you found it."

George hesitated, looked at the floor then at Trent.

"Let him go." Trent's voice was cold. "Get back outside with your buddies. Now."

George grumbled as he trudged away, but he went. One does not argue with a cop when he takes that tone. Well, I do, but that's different.

"Grace wants you to come to her house." Trent's voice had gone soft. Scary soft.

Chills darted down my spine. "I don't think so. I've got to do something with all the crazy people in my back yard."

"Fred's getting rid of them. You need to go to Grace. Something happened to Chuck."

"Something? What?"

"I don't know. Grace came running over, hysterical. She said he fell down and she can't wake him up. I called 911 and sent her home to wait for the EMTs, but she wants you."

"Me?" I squeaked. Grace and I weren't friends. We'd met when we thought our mutual ex, Rickhead, was dead. It had not been a bonding experience. Why did she want to see me now?

Chapter Two

A siren screamed from the street above.

"We need to go," Trent said.

I didn't want to know what brought the sirens shrieking into my neighborhood. I wanted to stay in the basement, hidden away from the lunatic crowd in my back yard and from whatever horrible thing had happened to Chuck.

But there was no chocolate in the basement. I'd have to leave eventually. Might as well be now.

Henry padded silently up the stairs. Trent and I followed.

Henry deserted us at the front door. I didn't blame him. The sirens had stopped, but I knew nothing good awaited us out there.

George's friends were racing helter-skelter toward the junker cars lining the street. Were they running because Fred had terrified them or because they heard the siren? At least they were leaving.

A fire truck sat in the street. Two men in clumsy gear ran toward Grace's house.

An ambulance screamed in from the other side and screeched to a stop. Three attendants rushed out.

Trent and I made it to Grace's front porch between the firemen and the EMTs.

I raised my hand to knock. Trent pushed through the door and strode inside.

A bit rude, but since the EMTs were right behind us, I followed.

Packing boxes surrounded a plaid sofa in the middle of the living room. A fireman pulled Grace away from the man lying motionless on that sofa.

Chuck.

The other fireman began CPR.

Grace flung herself into my arms. "He's not breathing!"

I patted her thin shoulder. "He'll be okay." I was pretty sure that was my second lie of the day. Chuck's body looked terribly still. He didn't seem to be responding to the efforts of the firemen.

The EMTs brought out electric paddles.

Not good.

"Let's go outside," Trent suggested.

Grace sobbed as she allowed me to lead her out.

I looked at Trent helplessly.

He looked at me helplessly.

Maybe Grace and I weren't friends, but her pain broke my heart. All I knew to do for pain was offer chocolate. That didn't seem appropriate at the moment.

"What happened?" I asked. "He was fine a few minutes ago. Wasn't he?"

Tears laced with mascara streamed down Grace's face. "I think he had a heart attack. He was carrying a big box. I shouldn't have let him carry such a big box!"

"It wasn't your fault," Trent assured her. "Did he have a history of heart problems?"

"He smoked! I knew it was going to kill him! He picked up that box and then he dropped it and grabbed his throat and fell down. I helped him get on the sofa.

18

He gasped and choked and..." She burst into sobs again.

A dark sedan parked at the curb. A man carrying a black bag got out and strode up the sidewalk. "Is this the residence of Chuck Mayfield?"

Grace lifted her tear-stained face. "That's my husband. Who are you?"

"I'm Dr. Richard Newton. I've been called to check on Mr. Mayfield."

"Okay." She started toward the door.

I stopped her. "Stay out here. Give him room to work."

The doctor disappeared inside.

"That's a good sign, isn't it?" she said. "That they called in a doctor."

I wasn't so sure. If a doctor could help Chuck, why hadn't the EMTs put him in their ambulance and rushed him to the hospital?

Grace turned to Trent. "Isn't it a good sign?" Desperation rose in her voice.

He shifted from one foot to the other. "It depends."

"I need to go in there." She reached for the door again.

It opened from within.

Dr. Newton stepped out. "Mrs. Mayfield—"

"Is he okay?" Grace interrupted.

"I'm sorry. Your husband...he's deceased."

Grace's hands flew to her throat. "You...he...he's..." She turned to me, eyes wide and frantic and filled with pain.

She'd been in love with Rickhead, and that had ended disastrously. Now she'd lost her new love. Life had not been fair to Grace.

"Was it a heart attack?" she asked. "He was lifting that heavy box and he used to smoke."

"I'm not sure at this point," Dr. Newton said. "We need to call in the police."

"The police?" Grace's incredulous response echoed my own thoughts. Chuck had collapsed. He hadn't been shot or stabbed.

"Yes, ma'am," the doctor said.

"Standard procedure for an unattended death with no obvious cause." Trent took out his wallet and showed his badge. "I'm a detective with the Pleasant Grove Police Department. I can take over."

"*Unattended*?" Grace repeated. "No. I was there."

"Let's go inside," Trent said.

Grace clutched my arm. "We've got to tell Rickie about his daddy. Lindsay, can you go get him? Please?"

"Of course." Not on my list of fun things to do, but at least it delayed going back into that house and seeing Chuck lying so still on that sofa.

I trudged across the street and returned to my back yard to find the guest of honor and his uninvited guests gone. One bright spot in the evening.

Fred, Sophie, Cathy, and Harold sat together on the patio, watching silently as I approached. All four clutched crystal glasses. Two wine bottles rested on the ground beside Fred's chair. Two bottles for the four of them? Not enough.

No one said a word, but I heard the question.

I shook my head.

Rickie sat at the patio table, his entire attention focused on his half-eaten burger.

The last rays of sun disappeared below the horizon. A shadowy cloud of silence settled over my back yard. Maybe over the entire world.

"Rickie." I flinched at how loud the word sounded. "Rickie," I said more softly, "your mother wants you to come home."

Rickie examined his burger carefully then took another bite.

In the distance an owl hooted his lonely, eerie call.

Sophie went to Rickie and put a hand on his shoulder. "Let's go see your mother."

He didn't look up. "I'm eating."

He must have heard his mother telling Trent something had happened to Chuck. The sirens meant that *something* was not good.

He was scared.

He didn't want to admit he was scared.

I could let him avoid it for a few more minutes. "Grace hasn't eaten. I need to put together some food for her."

"We moved everything inside." Cathy rose. "I'll help."

We entered the house and Henry butted my leg then showed me his empty food bowl. The home intrusion was forgotten. He never dwells on the past.

Cathy closed the door carefully behind us. "Rickie's father...step-father..."

"Dead." I filled Henry's bowl, focusing on those ugly, smelly pellets instead of Chuck's unmoving body and Grace's tear-stained face. "An unattended death. They don't know what happened."

"I see. There's a lot of food here. How much do you want to take over?" She peeled plastic wrap from a platter of hamburger patties.

"I don't know. There's just the two of them now. Half, I guess. Rickie's a growing boy." I got out plastic containers and bags. "Interesting custom, taking food to the bereaved family at a time when they have no appetite."

Cathy put half a dozen patties in a bowl and snapped on the lid. "It's why we do it. When our hearts are broken, we won't cook for ourselves. If someone else brings food, we're more likely to eat."

Cathy had lost a son. She knew whereof she spoke.

I zipped a bag of lettuce then paused. Cathy had also lost...in a different way...a grandson.

"This is probably none of my business," I said, "but should George be hanging around with those friends of his?"

Cathy shoved the container of meat into a shopping bag. "According to the terms of his parole, he should not be associating with convicted felons." She smoothed the bag and didn't look up. "We don't know that the men out there were convicted felons."

Maybe we didn't *know* it, but I'd have bet an entire week's supply of chocolate that they were. "He came with you and Harold. How did he leave? With one of them?"

"They all ran at the sound of the siren. George ran with them. I assume he'll be home eventually."

Would George be back in prison before the embers in the grill from his welcome home party turned to ashes?

22

Cathy filled a container with potato salad and put it into the bag.

It was my turn to speak. All of a sudden my blabbermouth went silent. I couldn't say anything positive about George's actions because I couldn't think of anything positive. Probably not a good idea to put my thoughts into words.

We finished packing food and went outside to find the only change was Rickie's empty plate. Sophie still stood beside him. Fred and Harold still held empty glasses.

"Lindsay's ready to take some food to your mother," Sophie said. "You'd better go with her."

"I want another cookie," he demanded.

"The cookies are going to your house. If you want a cookie, you can get your skinny butt in gear and follow them," I said.

I was once married to his father. I knew what worked. When cajoling fails, bully.

Rickie grumbled but slid from his chair.

"Do you want me to go with you?" Sophie asked.

Rickie studied the ground. "No."

I wouldn't have minded if everybody went. I had no idea how to comfort Grace or Rickie.

But Rickie was going to have a meltdown and didn't want anybody to witness the loss of his tough kid persona.

He probably didn't even want me there.

I didn't want to be there, but his mother wanted me.

"Thanks," I said, "but I'd really appreciate it if you all could finish cleaning up here before you go home."

Except for Rickie's empty plate and Fred's empty wine bottles, the area was spotless.

It was just an excuse. They all knew it.

I strode briskly across the street.

Rickie lagged behind.

The dark sedan, fire truck, and ambulance were gone.

I waited on the porch for Rickie to catch up then opened the door and let him enter first.

Grace shot across the room and pulled him into her arms. "Baby, it's your daddy!"

Rickie pushed her aside and ran from the room without looking at Chuck lying on the sofa or Trent sitting on one of the boxes with his ever-present notebook and pen.

Grace turned her mascara stained face to me. "Do you think I should go to him?"

She was asking me? The only experience I had with motherhood was a cat. I tried to think of what I'd do if Henry ran to his room after his stepfather died.

Henry is, as far as I know, an orphan, and he doesn't have a room. He owns the entire house.

In times of stress I give him catnip.

"I brought chocolate chip cookies." It was sort of the same thing. "And hamburgers. I'll take them to the kitchen."

She pulled a tissue from a half-empty box and pointed to a door on the far side of the room.

I went into a kitchen filled with boxes. Not only did Grace have to cope with Chuck's death, she would have to unpack alone, taking out each item she and Chuck had packed together.

I put the food in the refrigerator except for the cookies.

Should I take them to Rickie's room? He'd said he wanted one, but I wasn't sure he wanted me to deliver it.

Better I give them to Grace and let her deal with her son.

I returned to the living room to see Trent at the front door welcoming a new visitor. The tall woman with short brown hair carried a black bag. Another doctor?

"Donna Green," Trent said, "this is Grace Mayfield, wife of the deceased. Donna is one of our lab techs."

Lab tech?

She went to the sofa, set down her bag, and rummaged inside.

"Lindsay," Trent said brightly, "I see you have cookies. Why don't we go in the kitchen and let Donna work?"

Grace went first. I hung back so I could corner Trent. "Lab tech?" I hissed into his ear.

"Standard procedure for an unattended death with no obvious cause."

"You said that already. What does that mean?"

Had Chuck been murdered? No. I was being paranoid. Chuck had died in the arms of his wife.

Which didn't preclude murder.

"It means we have to gather all trace evidence at the scene and retain it until we know for sure the deceased died of natural causes."

Until we know for sure the deceased died of natural causes?

"Lindsay?" Grace's small voice sounded pitiful. She stood at the kitchen table, waiting for us to join her.

I pulled out the chair next to her and set my cookies on the table beside a packing box labeled *Kitchen*.

Trent sat across from her and laid his notebook on the table. Surely he wasn't going to question Grace like a suspect. I kicked him under the table.

He ignored me.

"Grace, can you tell me about any previous illnesses your husband had?"

She eased into a chair. "I don't know. He had a cold last winter."

"What kind of work did he do? Anything where he was exposed to chemicals?"

"He sold farm equipment to retail stores." She managed a weak smile. "He was so good, he had five states—Missouri, Kansas, Oklahoma, Nebraska, and Iowa."

"So he traveled?"

She wiped her eyes with a crumpled tissue. "He traveled a lot. Crappie Creek was too small to have a store, so he was always gone. He was going to find a job in Kansas City where he could stay home more."

"How long have you known Chuck?"

"Almost a year."

Almost a year?

"You got married in August," I said. "That's seven months ago."

Again the weak smile appeared. "He asked me to marry him on our second date. I said *yes* on our third. He told me he knew the minute he met me that I was the one, that he was going to marry me and spend the rest of his life with me."

No wonder the only illness she knew about was a cold last winter.

"Did he have any enemies?" Trent asked.

Enemies? Like somebody who might murder him?

I tried to read Trent's face to see what he was thinking. Stoic. He was entrenched in his cop persona.

"No!" Grace said. "Everybody liked Chuck."

"How about business rivals, other salesmen who might have resented his success?"

"Chuck didn't talk about his work. Why are you asking me all these questions?"

"Standard procedure," Trent replied.

If he asked whether she had an alibi for the time of death, I was going to hit him.

"Excuse me." Donna, the lab tech, stood in the kitchen doorway holding a vibrating cell phone. "This was in the deceased's pocket. Someone is calling him." She handed the phone to Trent.

Grace looked at the display. "Lutrell Tractor Supply. It's one of his stores. I can't talk to them right now. Lindsay, can you tell them?"

I shook my head but Trent handed me the phone anyway.

"Chuck Mayfield's office," I said.

A woman giggled. "Are you his new secretary? Honey, would you tell Chuck his wife wants to talk to him?"

27

Chapter Three

His wife?

It was a joke.

A very bad joke.

Thank goodness Grace hadn't taken the call.

I couldn't look at her.

The woman on the phone didn't know about Chuck's death. She didn't know her attempt at humor was inappropriate. I shouldn't feel so angry at her.

I dragged all my manners out of the closet and cleared my throat. "I regret to inform you that Chuck Mayfield cannot come to the phone. He died today in the arms of his wife." I couldn't stop myself from adding that last to let this idiot know how bad her behavior was.

Silence.

Had the woman hung up?

"That's not funny," she said.

"What do they want?" Grace asked.

"Nothing. Robo caller." I flinched as the stupid lie came out of my mouth.

"Let me talk to Chuck." The crazy woman's tone had turned belligerent.

"Do you have short term memory loss or bad hearing? I just told you why Chuck can't come to the phone."

Grace took the phone from me. "This is Chuck Mayfield's widow. Who is this?" Grace's eyes widened then narrowed. "You are one sick bitch, talking like that at a time like this." She disconnected the call. "Some people are just mean."

The phone vibrated.

Grace looked at the display. "It's her again."

Trent grabbed it. "This is Detective Adam Trent with the Pleasant Grove Police Department. Can I help you?—Ma'am—Ma'am, please calm down.—Ma'am, I assure you this is no joke." He listened a moment then gave the caller his badge number. "Feel free to report me. Would you like me to give you the number to call?—Chuck Mayfield cannot come to the phone. I personally heard the doctor pronounce him dead.—I am at Mr. Mayfield's home with his widow.—No, ma'am, I will not give you the address." He laid the phone on the table. "She hung up. If she calls again, Grace, don't answer."

Grace dabbed her swollen eyes with the damp tissue. "Why would that woman say she's Chuck's wife?"

"There are a lot of strange people out there," Trent said.

"She's calling from Lutrell Tractor Supply," Grace said. "She's using their phone. Do you think she broke into the store?"

I looked at Trent.

He looked at me.

"Was Chuck married before?" I asked.

"No! I'm the only woman he ever loved."

If they were both sixteen years old, I might have believed that. However, I wasn't going to upset Grace further by questioning Chuck's avowal of love. "It's

Saturday evening. Maybe there was an office party and that woman had too much to drink."

Trent gave a curt half-nod. As close as he could come to lying.

I reached for the phone.

Trent covered it with his hand. His eyes had that cop look.

"May I see that?" I used my most polite tone.

The only sound in the room was Grace sniffing.

"Why?" Trent asked.

"Why not?" I kept my gaze focused on Trent. "Grace, may I see Chuck's phone?"

"Yeah, sure."

Trent tried to stare me down. I could read his mind. Chuck's death was suspicious. The phone call from a woman claiming to be his wife was suspicious. He wanted to hang onto that phone.

But suspicious isn't the same thing as having a crime scene with bullet casings and blood spatter. He had no more right to that cell phone than I did.

"Missouri's a community property state," I said. "Grace owns half that phone, and she said I can look at her half."

Trent compressed his lips but slowly lifted his hand.

I took it, looked at the list of recent calls, memorized the number for Lutrell Tractor, then gave it to Grace.

Donna appeared in the kitchen doorway again. "I'm finished, Adam. Do you want to check anything before I call someone to take the body in for autopsy?"

Grace flinched at the clinical words.

"I'm done," Trent said. "Go ahead and call them."

We followed her to the living room and waited for someone to arrive and take away Chuck's body.

Grace sobbed.

Trent stood by stoically.

Rickie remained upstairs in his room.

Finally the body snatchers came and took Chuck away.

The sofa was empty. The house, crammed with boxes, felt empty. Grace's swollen eyes looked empty.

The evening had begun with a promise of disaster and had fulfilled that promise in a big way.

I wanted to be gone, to be safe in my house with Trent warm and alive beside me.

That desire felt selfish.

"Grace, is there anything we can do for you?" I asked. "Somebody you can call? Family? Your mother?"

"She's dead."

"How about your father?" Trent asked.

"Don't know who he is. I don't think Mama knew."

I was not friends with Grace. We got off to a bad start the first time she and Rickie showed up at the door of Death by Chocolate and conned me into letting them eat my food and spend the night at my house.

Nevertheless, my heart broke for her.

"Are you going to be okay?" I asked. "Do you and Rickie want to come over to my house?" Please say no!

Trent tensed. He wanted her to say no too. Saturday night was our night. He was wondering if I'd lost my mind. So was I.

"We'll be okay," Grace said. "Thank you for everything."

Trent edged toward the door.

I went to Grace and hugged her. She held on a bit convulsively for a moment.

"Well, okay," I said, "you have my phone number and you know where I live. Let me know if you need anything."

Trent took my hand as we walked away from Grace's house. The evening had turned to darkness and the spring warmth to a damp chill.

When we were safely inside my home, I grabbed Trent and held on tightly, probably a bit convulsively. I'd seen how easy it was to lose someone you love.

He returned my embrace. "I'm not going away. I'll be around for a very long time."

Having reassured myself he was still alive and breathing, I stopped trying to squeeze him like a boa constrictor. "Want me to warm up some burgers? Chocolate chip cookies only go so far."

"Sounds good."

He started into the kitchen with me, but I stopped him. "You cooked earlier. I'll bring you a beer. Sit. Relax. I've got this."

I took him a beer then returned to the kitchen, put a couple of hamburger patties in the microwave, and called Fred.

"How's Grace doing?" he asked.

"Terrible. Not bad enough her husband's dead, but he died by himself and they don't know why, Trent grilled Grace like she's a suspect, the lab tech came over to look for trace evidence, and Chuck has to be autopsied. It was awful."

"Are you trying to say there was an unattended death with no obvious cause which occasioned a visit from the forensics people, and Trent asked Grace for details?"

"You left out the part about the autopsy."

"That's standard procedure."

"Yeah, whatever. I didn't call you to have the oddities of our laws pointed out to me. I called you to find who belongs to a phone number. Some woman called Chuck's cell phone and said she was his wife. Chuck had the number in his phone as Lutrell Tractor Supply, one of the stores he deals with." I recited the digits.

"I'll call you back."

"Trent's here. I'll call you."

He hung up. I wasn't sure if he heard the last. Didn't matter. He'd know. He's psychic.

I gave Henry some catnip then put together burgers for Trent and me. We ate in the living room. I turned on the TV so we could pretend to watch and wouldn't have to talk. I didn't want to think about Grace sitting across the street with no mother, no father, and no husband...only her unpacked boxes and her once again fatherless son.

We finished our food and cuddled on the sofa. Henry strolled in and settled beside me.

Trent nuzzled the top of my head. "I'm sorry about your friend losing her husband."

"She isn't my friend." I thought about it. "I guess she's not my enemy anymore. Not that she ever really was my enemy. She was just kind of annoying. Her son's very annoying."

"I think all kids are at that age. Especially boys."

"Mmmm hmmm." I cuddled closer. It had been a long, harsh day. With my cat on one side and my boyfriend on the other, a warm blanket of contentment settled over me.

Trent took my almost empty Coke from my hand. "Your can is tilting dangerously."

"It's okay. A Coke stain would only look like another color flower on my sofa."

"I think my lady is getting sleepy. Want to go upstairs to bed?"

"Mmmm hmmm."

The three of us stood. Henry darted ahead.

He stopped at the front door.

It was almost midnight. Nobody could be at my door. "He probably wants to go out and look for mice," I said. I hoped.

Someone knocked.

No, no, no, no, no!

Nothing good could come from a knock at this hour.

"Lindsay?"

I was right.

It was Grace.

Trent opened the door.

Grace and Rickie. Rickie looked as if he'd been dragged from a deep sleep, the kind of sleep I would have been enjoying if they'd waited half an hour longer to knock.

"I saw your light was still on." Grace sounded timid and apologetic. She thrust a cell phone at Trent. "That woman keeps calling."

I snatched the phone from his hand before he could go into cop mode and keep it.

"Come in," I said. Not like I wanted to be upstairs snuggling with my boyfriend and my cat, drifting into peaceful slumber. "Have a seat and I'll get you something to drink."

Trent made a choking sound.

When someone comes to the door, it's polite to offer them something to drink, no matter the hour. Besides, it was an excuse to sneak off to the other room and find out if Fred knew anything about Grace's mysterious caller.

I darted into the kitchen and called him. "Are you awake?"

"I am now," he said.

"Did you find that phone number I gave you?"

"Yes."

"It's no tractor supply company, is it?"

"No. That phone number belongs to Stella Mayfield."

"Chuck's sister?" I knew it was a silly question. I was only delaying the inevitable.

"His wife."

So he'd lied to Grace about never being married before. "Ex-wife?"

"Wife. He married her three years ago, and I found no evidence they're divorced."

"Damn, damn, damn! Not bad enough he lied to Grace about her being his only love, she wasn't even his only wife!"

"It would appear Chuck was a bigamist."

"Maybe he had amnesia and didn't remember Stella. I've talked to the woman. I can see why he wouldn't want to remember her."

"If I have to choose between the possibility of Chuck having amnesia and Chuck lying, I'm afraid I'll have to opt for the latter."

I held the phone away from my ear and tried to melt it with my gaze. It didn't work. Fred was probably right. I put the phone back to my ear. "Grace is here. You need to come over and tell her about this."

"You have the information. Feel free to share it with her."

"No! I don't have any credibility. You need to talk to her. She'll have questions. You've seen the documents. You can answer her questions. I can't."

"You don't want to be the one to tell her."

Fred read my mind. I didn't want to cause Grace any more pain. "Please?"

"Do you have cookies?"

"Yes."

"All right."

He hung up.

Chuck had another wife. If she found out about Grace, would she have been angry enough to murder Chuck?

Not that I had any reason to think Chuck had been murdered.

Except having two wives put him in a potential-murder-victim category.

I set cookies on a plate, poured wine into glasses for Grace and me, then grabbed another beer for Trent and a Coke for Rickie. A hyperactive eleven-year-old boy did not need sugar and caffeine at midnight, but an eleven-year-old boy who'd just lost his bigamist step-father needed Coke and chocolate.

I returned to the living room.

36

Trent was in the recliner while Grace and Rickie occupied the sofa. Grace held Rickie close. He sat stiffly in her embrace, his expression obstinate as if he was too old for that sort of thing. But he wasn't pulling away.

She accepted a glass of wine with a shaky hand. Rickie brightened considerably at the Coke. I think he's an addict. I don't see that as a problem.

I put the cookies on the coffee table, handed the beer to Trent and perched beside him on the arm of the recliner.

He popped the top on his beer. "I showed Grace how to block that number. The police department will look into it on Monday."

"That's a great idea," I said. "But if we knew who the caller was, we might be able to stop her sooner."

"We've blocked the number," Trent said. "The woman's calls won't go through no matter who she is."

"I just meant—"

Saved by the knock on the door.

I stood.

"Wait..." Trent was right behind me.

I beat him to the door and flung it open. "Fred! What a nice surprise! Come in and have some cookies."

He hesitated.

I winked to let him know that I hadn't really forgotten he was coming. A conspiratorial wink.

"Do you have something in your eye?" he asked.

Men! "Come in." I turned and bumped into Trent.

"Hey, Fred."

"Good evening, Detective Trent."

I turned to Grace. "I think Fred has some information we may need to discuss."

Trent leveled his gaze on me. "How do you know he has information if his arrival was a surprise?"

Cops weren't supposed to use their detective skills on their girlfriends.

I took a seat next to Grace. She was going to need support and I needed some distance from Trent for a few minutes, enough time for him to forget my slight subterfuge about Fred's arrival. I hoped Fred's astonishing news would displace all else in Trent's mind.

Trent returned to the recliner, and Fred stood just inside the door. All eyes focused on him. He clasped his hands. He clenched his jaw. I'd never seen Fred uncomfortable before. "Grace," he finally said, "I have some details about the woman who's been calling you." He paused, unclasped his hands and moved them behind his back. "That number does not belong to Lutrell Tractor Supply. It belongs to a woman who lives in Moberly, Missouri."

"Lutrell Tractor Supply's in Moberly," Grace said.

"Yes, but their number is different. This woman's name is Stella Mayfield. She and Charles Dean Mayfield were married three years ago."

Grace gasped. "Chuck was divorced?"

"They never divorced," Fred continued. "Your husband was a bigamist."

Silence.

Lots of dark, oppressive silence.

Rickie shot up, burst past Fred, and ran out the door. He took his Coke with him. He'd be okay.

"No. That's not true." Grace spoke so quietly I barely heard her words.

"It is true," Fred assured her.

She rose slowly, a woman in a trance. "No. Chuck loved me." She speared Fred with a look of pure loathing. "Why would you say something like that? You're meaner than that woman! You go to hell!"

She charged out the door.

"I'll be sure she gets home all right." Trent followed her.

I looked at Fred. "That went well."

"About as well as I expected."

Sally Berneathy

Chapter Four

A night spent with Trent is always good, but my antique bed was too small to accommodate four of us...me, Trent, Henry, and Grace's dilemma. I could have shoved Henry out of bed, but I couldn't stop obsessing about Grace. Unfortunately my obsessions tend to pour out through my mouth. When Trent and Henry both began snoring, I had to obsess silently. That was tough.

Life had not dealt kindly with Grace. Her mother was dead, she didn't know who her father was, she'd been Rickhead-ized, then Chuck died on her and posthumously revealed he'd betrayed her.

My crazy life was smooth in comparison.

Finally I slept and dreamed about Chuck surrounded by women of all shapes and sizes in bridal gowns.

The next day after a late brunch of leftovers, Trent went home and Henry went out to patrol his territory.

I closed the door behind them and pondered whether I should go to Grace's to console her, go next door to Paula's to update her, or go to Fred's to see if he'd found out anything else about Chuck's other wife.

Be a good neighbor? Share the gossip? Try to find out more gossip?

Share the gossip won. Paula needed to know what was happening right across the street from her.

I opened my front door.

40

George stood on my porch holding a bouquet of slightly wilted flowers. He smiled.

I frowned.

He extended the flowers to me.

I made no move to take them.

"I wanted to apologize for yesterday," he said.

I groaned deep inside. An apology, however false, must be accepted. "Apology accepted. Good-bye." I started to close the door.

He grabbed the door frame. "No, wait! Please, I brought you flowers to show I'm sorry. I didn't know my friends would be so rowdy."

"I'm allergic to flowers." Yes, it was a lie, but he started it. Didn't know his friends would be so rowdy? Please!

I slammed the door on his hand.

He cursed and yanked his fingers away.

I closed and locked the door.

He knocked again. "My grandma and grandpa are real upset with me," he yelled. "I just want to make this right."

What he wanted was another chance to dig up my basement and look for the drug money he'd hidden there. The condition of his flowers indicated he might have been waiting all morning for Trent to leave. I had no idea how much longer he'd stay.

I went out through the kitchen. As I made my way to Paula's back door, I peeked around the bushes and saw an older model beige sedan parked in front of my house. I would not go home until that car was gone.

I knocked on Paula's back door then made faces while she peered through the peephole, took off the chain, and unlocked both deadbolts. With her ex in prison for the rest of his life, she's not as paranoid as she used to be, but old paranoia dies hard.

"Come in," she invited. "I'd ask why you're using the back door, but I probably don't want to know."

"You don't, but I'm going to tell you anyway."

"Anlinny!" Zach rushed up and flung his arms around me, almost toppling me. The kid's growing. He grabs me around my thighs now, an improvement over grabbing me around my knees.

I tousled his soft hair. He's going to be tall like his worthless dad, but his blond hair, blue eyes, and sweet temperament come from his mother. "Hi, Hot Shot."

He looked up. "Uncle Matthew got me a truck that goes all by itself and it has a real horn. Did you bring cookies?"

"Sorry, no cookies today." Kid gets his chocolate addiction from his Aunt Lindsay. I'm glad I can have a positive influence on a growing child.

"Go play with your new truck." Paula turned him toward the living room.

"Okay." He ran from the room, short legs churning.

"Does he ever walk?" I asked.

"Only when it's time to go to bed or take a bath. Then he drags along very slowly." She sat in a chair at the kitchen table. "Tell me about George's party."

She'd turned down an invitation to that party. She didn't want her four-year-old son around criminals. I didn't blame her. Instead, she and Matthew, the man she'd been tentatively involved with for about a year, had taken Zach to the park. After her experience with Zach's father, it was taking her a while to trust again. Matthew was patient.

I slumped into a chair across from her. "The party was a nightmare, and things went downhill from there." I told her about George's friends diverting me while George snuck down to the basement. "As soon as Trent left this morning, George showed up at my door with half-dead flowers, trying to con his way inside again."

Paula grimaced. "Too bad you don't know where that money went so you can tell him and get rid of him."

She suspected that I knew, but I was keeping the secret. That's not an easy thing for me to do.

I changed the subject. "Rickhead bought the house across the street from you, and he's renting it to Grace and her new husband, Chuck, except yesterday Chuck died an unattended death so it's just Grace and Rickie, and we found out Chuck's a bigamist."

"You lost me right after Grace and Chuck renting the house."

A large green truck zoomed into the kitchen and honked. And honked and honked and honked.

"Zachary!" Paula said.

Zach came into the room holding a remote control and giggling.

"Stop making so much noise or you're going to be in big trouble," Paula warned.

The truck quit honking, but Zach didn't quit giggling. He doesn't find his mother very intimidating. He's never seen her go up against a psycho. I have.

"Take your truck back to the living room," she said.

He ran to my side and laid his head in my lap, still giggling.

43

"Hey, Hot Shot, you better do what your mother says or she may spank you."

We both giggled at that.

Zach and his truck zoomed into the living room.

I gave Paula more details about the events of the previous day.

She sighed. "I liked it better when you talked fast and jumbled everything together. It sounds like we may have a murderer living across the street."

"Stop that. We don't know Chuck was murdered, but even if he was, we know Grace didn't do it."

"We do?"

"Yes, we do. You should have seen the way she looked at him. She loved him. She was heart-broken when he died, and very upset when she found out about his other wife."

Zach zoomed back into the room and over to his mother. "Mommy, I'm hungry. I want ice cream."

Paula wrapped her arms around him. "How about a grilled cheese sandwich instead?"

"Anlinny wants ice cream," he said.

"Aunt Lindsay has already eaten," I said. "Maybe later."

"Okay." He scampered back into the living room.

Paula rose and went to the refrigerator.

I went to the window on the side of the kitchen. The trees were budding, but I could see the street in front of my house. George's car was still there. I wanted to avoid going home until he left. "I think I'll check on Grace."

Paula stood with a loaf of bread in one hand and a package of cheese in the other. "You need to think about what you said."

"That Zach can have ice cream later? You know you'll give in."

"You said Grace was very upset when she found out Chuck had another wife."

"Duh."

"Upset enough to kill him?"

"No!"

"Perhaps you shouldn't visit her alone."

Paula really is a nice person, but sometimes she's a little overly-cautious about people. She used to be a lot overly-cautious. I knew her for a year before she finally told me she'd killed her husband. Well, she hadn't really killed him, but she thought she did. Who keeps a secret like that? If I'd killed Rickhead, I'd have taken out a billboard on I-70 inviting everyone to party in my jail cell.

I went out Paula's front door and ran across the street to Grace's house as fast as I could in case George was watching.

Grace wasn't crying when she answered the door. A good sign.

"Come in, Lindsay. A friend of yours is here helping me unpack."

A friend? I didn't have that many friends. It wasn't Paula. I'd just left her. Not likely Fred. Maybe Sophie.

Grace stepped back and held the door open.

At the end of the plaid sofa where Chuck had died yesterday George Murray clutched a cardboard box and looked guilty.

"What's he doing here?" I demanded.

"George brought me some flowers. He said the living should enjoy flowers." Grace bit her lip.

"Because the dead person at the funeral can't." Tears flooded her eyes.

"And he's helping you unpack? How sweet." What was George up to? I wanted to tell her that he wasn't my friend, he wasn't her friend, that she couldn't trust him, and that he'd brought me the flowers first which certainly proved she couldn't trust him.

But Grace had been dealt enough reality blows lately. The best I could do was to mitigate whatever con George was working.

I gave him my you're-in-big-trouble-now look. It had the same effect on him that it has on Henry. None.

"George said he knew how hard it would be for me to come across Chuck's things while I'm unpacking," Grace said, "so he's helping."

A sheen of perspiration appeared on George's forehead. "Yeah, uh, I remember when I lost my mom and dad. It's tough going through their—you know—pictures and clothes and stuff."

Pictures and clothes and stuff? What was George looking for in Chuck's pictures and clothes and stuff?

Was he searching for something so important he'd murdered Chuck to get it?

How could I get him out of there without upsetting Grace?

I'd have to make up a story, which isn't the same thing as lying. Ask Michael Connelly or Patricia Cornwell or Sara Paretsky.

"Your cell phone must be turned off, George," I said. "Your grandmother called me. She needs you to come home right away."

46

His eyes narrowed. "My cell phone's on. She could have called me."

"Cell phones are so unreliable. Maybe you need to change your provider."

Grace went to his side. "You go on home. I'll be fine. Thank you so much for helping."

"I'm always glad to help." George's soft voice was in direct contradiction to the threat in his eyes when he looked at me. "Maybe after I take care of whatever Nana wants, I could pick up a pizza and come back. Your kid like pizza?"

Grace beamed. "Rickie loves pizza. So do I."

"I'll put this box in the bedroom for you. I'm sure Nana can wait another five minutes." He climbed the stairs.

I followed.

He turned into the first bedroom. I stopped in the doorway. He set the box on a dresser and slit the tape.

"What the hell are you up to?" I demanded.

He spun around, a knife in his hand. "I'm trying to be a nice guy. What the hell are you up to?"

I gulped and took a step backward.

Surely he wouldn't use that knife on me with Grace downstairs.

"You need to mind your own business and stay out of mine." He folded the knife and put it in his pocket.

Whew.

He pushed past me.

I didn't try to stop him. Instead I looked around the bedroom to figure out what he'd been doing.

The room looked ordinary. A queen size bed with a bookcase headboard. A dresser and two chests of drawers, not matched, not new. Unopened boxes were stacked along one wall with empty boxes along the other.

I looked inside the box George had opened. Men's clothing.

"You don't like him, do you?"

I spun around. I hadn't heard Grace come in. "He just got out of prison."

"He told me. Everybody makes mistakes. Reckon I've made a few myself."

That reminded me... "Where's Rickie?"

"In his room, playing on his computer. He's pretty tore up about Chuck dying, but he doesn't like to admit it." She wrapped her arms around herself. "My little boy is growing up. It would have been good for him to have a dad."

"Yeah." Too bad the sperm donor, Rickhead, was such a sorry excuse for a father. He was also a sorry excuse for a human being, but that's another story.

"George said I shouldn't believe that woman who claims to be married to Chuck. He said she's just trying to cause trouble. Probably an old girlfriend, somebody he dumped when he met me."

I opened my mouth to protest that Fred had found the marriage certificate then closed it without speaking. Did it really matter? Chuck was dead. If it made Grace feel better to believe he loved only her, what did it hurt?

I turned back to the box George had set on the dresser. "I'll help you unpack."

"Thanks. It is pretty hard, finding one of Chuck's shirts or a picture of us. I miss him so much."

Whatever George was planning, I was going to stop him. I would not let him make Grace's life any worse. "This appears to be a box of his clothes. Does it need to be unpacked or, uh...?" Maybe too soon to suggest donating his clothes to charity.

Someone knocked loudly on the front door.

Had George come back? "I'll go."

"It's okay. I'll get it."

We raced down the stairs and through the living room toward the front door.

I have longer legs.

I yanked open the door. A blond Amazon with tightly clenched lips stood there.

"I'm Stella Mayfield!" She punched me in the jaw.

Chapter Five

I staggered backward into the house.

Grace flew past me and head-butted the woman who was easily twice her size.

They fell into a mass of arms and legs.

Somebody screamed.

Somebody cursed.

I got my balance and started outside to help Grace. The Amazon—Stella Mayfield—would annihilate her.

Before I got through the door, Rickie shoved me aside and dove into the fray.

The cursing and screaming intensified.

Now I had to save Grace and Rickie both.

I grabbed the door frame, righted myself again, and charged out.

Stella was on her back with Grace on top of her, pulling her hair with one hand and punching her in the face with the other. Rickie had a foot on her thigh and was yanking her leg upward with both hands, bending the knee the wrong way.

Clearly I wasn't needed except maybe to save Stella who was doing most of the screaming.

I tapped Rickie on the shoulder. "Um, maybe you shouldn't be doing that so hard. You could break her leg."

Rickie grinned and gave an extra tug.

Stella screamed louder.

"Bitch deserves it, saying she's married to my daddy."

Rickie's inappropriate language was appropriate for the occasion.

I moved closer to Grace but not so close she might accidentally hit me. "I think you won. You should probably let her up now."

She didn't even glance at me. "You want to take a swing? I bet your jaw hurts."

Yes, it hurt, but I didn't have a clue how to throw a punch. Besides, I didn't want to damage the hands that create chocolate masterpieces.

"No, you go ahead. But remember, if you kill her, you'll go to jail."

Grace got to her feet, straddling Stella but not hitting her anymore.

Stella put her hands over her face and screamed again.

Rickie hadn't stopped torturing her leg.

Grace stepped away from the woman, put a hand on her son's shoulder, and gave a brief nod. He released Stella's leg, stood, kicked her and called her another bad name.

Stella sat up cautiously.

"Who the hell are you?" Grace demanded. "What are you doing here and why did you hit my friend?"

Her friend? Was she talking about me?

Stella wiped blood from her mouth with the back of her hand and squinted at me through swollen eyes. "I'm Chuck Mayfield's wife."

Grace drew back her fist. "I'm Chuck Mayfield's wife."

The woman looked at me. "Then who are you?"

"I'm not Chuck Mayfield's wife."

She turned to Grace, her dark eyes slits of fury. "You're the one who said all those awful things to me on Facebook." She struggled to her feet, clutching the porch rail for support.

Grace balled her fists. "I'm not on Facebook."

Rickie stepped forward. "It was me. I tracked you down, you lying—"

"You tracked her down?" Grace asked.

"Wasn't hard."

Grace beamed at her son. "You're so smart." She frowned. "You tell her where we live?"

He straightened defiantly. "She's got to apologize for calling you and telling you those lies."

Psychic prediction...that wasn't going to happen.

Grace turned back to Stella. "You the crazy woman that's been calling from Luttrell Tractor?"

Stella moved her head from side to side, the movement a mixture of uncertainty and pain. "I called my husband while I was sitting on our sofa in our house. Luttrell's one of my husband's accounts."

Grace stiffened. "My husband sold farm machinery to Luttrell."

"My husband sells farm machinery to Luttrell."

Grace and Stella glared at each other.

"Let's hit her some more, Mama," Rickie said.

"Maybe it's a different Chuck Mayfield," I suggested. I didn't believe that, but I didn't want to see another fight.

"How long you been married?" Grace asked.

"Three years. How long you been married?"

"Not quite a year."

Silence.

I clapped my hands. "Hey, I've got a great idea! Let's all have a Coke and chill out. If you don't have any cold Cokes, Grace, I've got plenty at my house."

Nobody seemed enthusiastic about my idea of a peace drink.

"Must be a different Chuck Mayfield," I said again. "It's a common name. Let's all forget this ever happened."

"Show her your wedding picture, Mama. I'll get it." Rickie darted into the house. The screen door slammed behind him.

The two women continued to glare at each other.

Another prediction...when Stella saw her husband in Grace's wedding picture, World War III was going to erupt.

I thought briefly of running home and hiding, leaving the two of them to fight it out. But Grace had called me her friend. She'd attacked the woman who punched me. I had to stand by her in this no-win situation.

I prayed for a distraction...a small tornado going down the middle of the street, a vegetarian lion running amuck, a major eclipse of the sun.

Same success as when I pray for the winning lottery ticket.

Rickie came out with an eight-by-ten picture frame. The screen door slammed behind him.

He handed the picture to Grace.

She looked at it closely as if seeing it for the first time.

I grabbed it from her. "I've never seen your wedding picture, Grace! What a pretty dress."

"It's my waitress uniform. We didn't have a fancy wedding."

"Neither did we." Stella reached for the picture.

I moved backward, up the porch steps, holding it away from her.

She had longer arms than I realized. She grabbed one side of the frame. "Give it to me."

"I'm not through looking at it."

She yanked the frame from me.

I held my breath.

Nobody moved.

Even the infamous Kansas City wind that never stops blowing held its breath.

Finally she gave the picture to Grace and took a cell phone from the back pocket of her jeans. She scrolled through a few screens then handed it to Grace.

I leaned over and saw a picture of Stella and Chuck.

Grace's knuckles turned white as she clutched the phone.

Rickie snatched it out of her hand. "That man's not my daddy. He doesn't look anything like my daddy."

Grace looked at me, eyes filled with hope.

I couldn't betray that hope. "I think Rickie's right," I said. "See the distance between the eyes? That's critical when they do the facial recognition thing on TV. In this cell phone picture, the distance is only about an eighth of an inch. It's closer to half an inch in Grace's picture."

The two women looked at each other then back at me.

54

"My picture's bigger," Grace said. Her voice was low with defeat, but her eyes still held that desperate need to believe.

"Well, um, it's all in the perspective." That made no sense, but I'd run out of blarney.

Grace slumped onto the top porch step.

Stella sank beside her.

Rickie threw her cell phone at her. "I hate you!"

The phone bounced off her shoulder and landed in the grass. She didn't seem to notice.

Rickie ran back in the house.

The screen door slammed behind him.

"He said I was the only woman he'd ever loved." The small voice coming from Stella's not-so-small body sounded strange.

"He told me the same thing," Grace said.

"I don't understand," Stella said.

I understood. The man was a lying, cheating bigamist scum.

I refrained from expressing my opinion.

"Them people on the phone said Chuck's dead. Is that true?" Stella asked.

Grace drooped lower. "Yeah."

"What happened? He never got sick."

Grace sniffled. "I don't know. We were unpacking and he just fell over."

I needed to leave and let the two wives-in-law figure things out for themselves. Stella seemed as confused as Grace about Chuck's double life. Unlikely she killed him.

But I was on the porch, and they were on the steps. I'd have to ask them to move aside. I didn't want to interrupt them. More importantly, I didn't want to draw their attention to me.

Maybe I should go inside Grace's house and out the back door.

I didn't want to encounter Rickie.

"Your boy called him daddy," Stella said.

"Chuck was going to adopt him. His real daddy signed the papers. We were going to see the judge on Monday."

Stella snorted. "We were trying to have a baby. It would have been his kid, not some other man's."

"He couldn't have kids. He had a football injury."

Football? It was hard to imagine skinny Chuck playing football.

Stella looked smug. "He never played football. He lied to you."

"How many babies you had?" Grace asked.

Stella hunched forward and wrapped her arms around her knees. "None."

"Maybe he lied to you."

"Maybe."

The fighting was over. Time for me to go but, short of levitating over their heads, I had to make one of them move.

Rickie came outside.

The screen door closed quietly behind him.

"That man's phone is ringing again."

That man's phone? Chuck was no longer Daddy. Nobody moved.

I took the phone from him and looked at the display. Higgins Farm Machinery. A Kansas area code.

I accepted the call, put the phone to my ear, and grunted in an effort to sound like a typical man.

"Hi, sweetie pie. When you coming home?"

I stared at the phone in horror. Not another one! Was Chuck a trigamist?

I looked up at the silent people around me.

Rickie turned away and went inside.

Grace and Stella sat frozen in place on the porch steps.

"What states did you say Chuck's territory included?" I asked.

"Missouri," Stella said. "And Kansas."

"Oklahoma, Nebraska, and Iowa," Grace added.

Two wives in Missouri, maybe one in Kansas. Had he branched out to Oklahoma, Nebraska, and Iowa as well?

"Who was that on the phone?" Grace asked.

"Higgins Farm Machinery." Once again no earthquake, tsunami, or tornado appeared to save me. I was going to have to tell Grace the truth. "I'm not sure who the caller was, but she wanted to know when sweetie pie would be home."

"Higgins Farm Machinery," Stella repeated quietly. "That's one of his clients."

"In Hutchinson, Kansas," Grace said.

I offered the phone to her. "We should probably go through Chuck's list of contacts and see how many clients he has."

Grace sat on her hands. "You do it."

Stella folded her hands in her lap. "Yeah, you."

I did it.

There were twenty-six.

Twenty-six suspects?

Grace's number was listed under Maxwell Mowers and More.

"Surely Chuck isn't married to twenty-six women," I said. "Some of these places must be legitimate."

"We can call those numbers and see who answers," Grace said.

"Good idea." Again I extended the phone to her.

"I can't stand to hear one more woman say she's married to my husband."

I offered the phone to Stella.

"You do it. You weren't married to him."

"She's right," Grace agreed. "You have to do it."

I'd won the election and I hadn't even entered the race.

"All right," I said, "I'll find out who belongs to these phone numbers."

But not by calling them.

This was a job for the Fred-man.

Chapter Six

I offered Fred chocolate chip cookies in exchange for tracking down all those numbers on Chuck's phone. He asked for brownies as well. We struck a bargain for cookies and brownies. I got a deal. He didn't know I was willing to go cookies, brownies, and Shannon's Double Chocolate Double Caramel Cake.

When Trent called that evening, I spent the first ten minutes telling him about my confrontations with George and Stella.

"The woman hit you? Are you okay?"

His concerned tone sent sparkles through my heart. He was worried about me. He cared about me. "I'm fine. A little sore." I tried to sound brave and strong but wounded at the same time.

"How about Grace and Rickie? Were they hurt?"

My sparkles dulled. Grace had no one to worry if she'd been hurt in the fight. The man who would have worried about her was dead. Worse, he was the cause of the fight.

"They're all right, but both of them are upset. Rickie has stopped calling Chuck his father. Now he's just that man."

"I'm sorry to hear that."

"I'll take her more chocolate tomorrow."

"Good idea. But if George comes to her house while you're there, don't confront him again. Go home, call me, call Fred, call 911…just stay away from that man."

"Grace shouldn't be alone with him. I don't trust him."

"I don't either. That's why you need to stay away from him."

We needed to stay away from that subject. Next thing I knew, Trent was going to be asking me to promise to stay away from George, and I couldn't do that. I had to protect Grace from him. "I have to go. Henry wants catnip." It wasn't a lie. Henry always wanted catnip.

"Lindsay, listen to me, please. George is a dangerous man."

"I know. I'll be careful. Love you."

He sighed. "Love you too. If you get in trouble, you have my number."

Trent knows me too well.

༂

The next day I lost myself in serving chocolate to the masses and was able to put Grace's dilemma out of my mind for a few hours.

When I arrived home, King Henry greeted me at the door, half-dead from starvation.

Sometimes my cat's a little melodramatic.

I poured food into his bowl and he dove in, crunching loudly.

I got a fresh Coke and went into the living room to relax.

Someone knocked…light, rapid knocks.

Probably not George.

I opened the door.

Grace stood on my porch, hands clenched, eyes wide. "Chuck was murdered!"

"Why do you think that?"

"The cops were here all afternoon."

I was dating a cop, but I was the last to hear when somebody got murdered? They spent the afternoon across the street from my house, but I had to learn about it from a neighbor? Had Trent known about Chuck's murder when we'd talked the night before?

He had. That's why he'd been so adamant that I avoid George. Did that mean George was a suspect?

"Come in. Would you like a Coke? A glass of wine?" I looked behind her. "Where's Rickie?"

"Sophie came over after the cops left and asked if she could take him for ice cream." Grace crossed the room and sank onto my sofa with a sigh. "Yeah, I could use some wine. You got any of that pink stuff? I really like the pink stuff."

I went to the kitchen, poured half a glass for me and a full glass for Grace.

She accepted her drink. "Thank you."

Grace had much better manners than Trent's ex who had sneered at my choice of wine. I'm a connoisseur of chocolate and only drink real Coke, but when it comes to wine...those boxes fit much better in my refrigerator and have a handy spigot. And it tastes just fine to me, especially the pink stuff.

I sat in my arm chair. "Chuck was...?" I couldn't bring myself to say the m word in front of her. "He didn't die from natural causes?"

Tears gathered in her eyes. "He was poisoned."

"Poisoned?" My gut clenched. He'd been at my house minutes before he died. I'd given him a cookie. "Was he allergic to nuts?"

"No, he loved nuts. Why?"

"I thought maybe...I mean...nobody else at the party died so I thought he might..." Shut up, Lindsay! "I'm sorry. What kind of poison?"

"Cyanide." The tears spilled from her eyes and rolled down her cheeks. "And they think I did it!"

"I'm sure they don't think that." A white lie. The spouse is always the first suspect, and the suspicion likely increased with the number of spouses. I could only hope they wouldn't put Grace, Stella, and Higgins Farm Machinery in the same prison cell. That could bring on another murder. Or two.

She wiped at her tears. No mascara today. "It was horrible. They asked me all kinds of questions. They know about Stella."

I flinched. "Trent probably blabbed. I'm sorry. Sometimes he takes that cop thing too far."

"It's okay. They were bound to find out. They searched the house, went through all the boxes that weren't unpacked already, and made a big mess."

"Cops can be real pigs."

"Trent told them to put things back the way they found them. I told them not to bother. I have to get everything unpacked and organized for Rickie's sake. He was supposed to start his new school today, but I couldn't make him face a bunch of strangers when his daddy just died." She took a long drink of wine and looked forlorn. "Well, he was almost Rickie's daddy."

"He was Rickie's father. Having the judge approve those papers was a technicality." I couldn't believe the words that came out of my mouth. Had I really stood up for the bigamist jerk?

The grateful expression on Grace's face told me I'd said the right thing even if I'd told a lie.

Maybe it wasn't a lie. Who knew what was going on in Chuck's mind?

"The cops want his phone. I told them I gave it to you because I didn't want it around with Stella's messages and all. Rickie said he can erase those phone numbers and messages before we give it to the cops. Did you find out if there's any more..." She swallowed. "Any more of them?"

"Fred's checking. I'll call him."

She sat forward. "Fred? He knows about the others?"

Had she hoped to keep Chuck's duplicity a secret? Pleasant Grove's a small town. A murdered bigamist would be the hottest new story since Mrs. Henderson's registered poodle gave birth to a litter that strongly resembled Mr. Johnson's rescue dog next door. "It's okay. Fred's much better at keeping secrets than Trent."

I took my phone from the pocket of my jeans and tapped his name.

The strains of classical music came from outside.

The music stopped.

Fred answered the phone. "I'm on your front porch."

Should have known Fred would have classical music for his ring tone. "Come in. The door's unlocked." Not that a locked door would stop Fred.

My psychic (or psychotic) cat streaked across the room and exited the house as Fred entered. As usual, they ignored each other.

"Good afternoon, Grace. I noticed you had a rough day."

"It wasn't much fun."

I stood. "We're having wine. Can I bring you some?"

He looked at my glass and shuddered. "No, thank you."

"I have chocolate chip cookies."

"Yes, thank you."

"Have a seat. Don't start without me."

I hurried to the kitchen and returned with a plate of cookies.

They had started without me. Fred sat next to Grace on the sofa. She clutched a cell phone and regarded Fred with wide eyes.

He glanced up when I set the cookies on the coffee table then returned his attention to Grace. "Some of the entries were dealers. Chuck transacted business deals with them."

"He was good at his job," Grace said proudly. "He was a top salesman."

"Actually, his sales placed him at the bottom of the pyramid."

Grace's lower lip trembled. "No. He made good money. He took care of me and Rickie."

"You were moving to a house owned by your ex."

"Chuck wanted to pay Rick for the house. He said we didn't need anything from him, but Rick wanted to be sure we couldn't come after him for back child support when Chuck adopted Rickie. Rick doesn't trust people."

"We judge others by our own standards," I said.

"What?" Grace asked.

"Rick isn't trustworthy so he thinks nobody else is."

"Chuck had no money problems?" Fred ignored my profound observation.

"No." She held up her left hand to display a gold band and a ring with a stone so large I'd assumed it was glass. Maybe crystal. Maybe not. "He bought me and Rickie anything we wanted."

"Did you see his tax returns?" Fred asked.

"Of course not. That wasn't any of my business."

I couldn't decide if I was more aghast at Grace's assertion that she didn't consider her husband's tax returns any of her business or the notion that not even the IRS could hide from Fred. "Fred, did you see his tax returns?"

Fred arched an indignant white eyebrow. "Are you suggesting I hacked into the IRS database?"

"Yes, and I'm impressed."

"Grace, your husband's income as an independent farm machinery salesman was barely above poverty level. Did you actually see evidence of money, or is it possible Chuck was bragging? Maybe he offered to buy the house from Rick because he knew he wouldn't have to."

"No!" Grace bristled. "He had money! I saw it."

"You saw what? Bank account records?"

"Chuck didn't trust banks. He had cash. Lots of cash."

"Cash," Fred repeated. "He had $42 in his wallet."

Grace's jaw tightened. "He had more."

"I found five additional wives, all of whom have low-paying jobs yet live in decent homes."

Grace went eerily still.

"Grace? Are you okay?"

"Five?" she whispered. "Five besides Stella and me?"

"Yes. Going solely on the data available in his cell phone, Chuck Mayfield was married to seven women. You and Stella in Missouri, two in Kansas, one in Iowa, one in Nebraska, and one in Oklahoma. I've only checked the numbers on his cell phone, so that may not be the complete list."

"Not the complete list?" Grace repeated Fred's words in horror.

Fred's a brilliant man, but sometimes he doesn't have a clue.

"Grace, eat a cookie," I ordered. Chocolate is the universal remedy for shock.

"Not the complete list?" she said again.

I picked up a cookie from the plate and extended it toward her. "Eat. Now."

She accepted the cookie and bit off a tiny piece then swallowed without chewing. At least she got a little chocolate into her system.

"There may be more of those women out there?" she asked.

The chocolate had given her the power to speak coherently.

"We don't know that," I said before Fred could make the situation worse by giving her further information.

"Since the police are involved, I'm sure they'll find out. Do you want me to check first so you'll be prepared?" Fred did have some sensitivity after all.

Grace jerked her head from side to side. "No. Rickie's going to erase those numbers from Chuck's phone, and the police won't know about anybody but Stella."

I'm not averse to a little bit of evidence tampering now and then, but I didn't think this was one of those times when it would be beneficial. "Grace, you're a suspect in Chuck's murder. It would not be a good idea to erase those numbers. You need to give them as many suspects as possible."

She laid the offending phone on the coffee table and took a drink of wine. A long drink. "One of those women killed my Chuck because he married me and was leaving her."

I sent Fred a telepathic message, daring him to contradict Grace's theory.

His expression remained serene, innocent as a murderer on death row. "The authorities will be able to access all Chuck's cell phone records. Erasing the data on the phone would be ineffective as well as suspicious."

"Everybody's going to know about all those women no matter what I do?"

"Yes." Fred selected the most symmetrical cookie on the plate.

"He loved me," Grace said. "He told me I was the only woman he ever really loved."

He'd told Stella the same thing. Probably the other women too.

"We know he loved you," I assured her, "but when somebody's murdered, the dirty laundry comes out."

"I wash all our clothes every week."

Fred choked.

I refused to look at him. "It's an expression. It means all the secrets will come out."

"Do you think Stella killed him? I kind of like her after our fight and all."

Stella and Grace friends? That was beyond weird.

"What was in that box George Murray took from your house early this morning?" Fred asked.

George had been at Grace's house again, and he'd left with something. I looked at Grace to see how she was taking Fred's question.

Guilty.

That was the only word to describe her expression.

"Did George come by to help you unpack?" I asked.

"Yes." She sat rigidly upright, clutching her half-empty wine glass so tightly it would have broken if it had been crystal instead of plastic.

Definitely guilty.

Fred waited. He was doing that thing the cops do...ask a question and say nothing until the guilty party confesses.

What was Grace feeling so guilty about? She would be guilty of bad taste if she'd begun some kind of relationship with George Murray, but bad taste in men wasn't a crime. If it was, they'd have hanged me for marrying Rickhead.

I should follow Fred's lead and be quiet, wait for Grace to confess.

I didn't.

"Grace, you've gone through a terrible trauma, losing your husband like that. It would be normal to, uh, look for companionship." But not with George Murray! Please say that wasn't what happened!

Grace's eyes widened in horror. "What are you saying? I'd never cheat on Chuck!"

"What was in the box George took with him early this morning?" Fred's repetition of the question was casual and non-threatening, but it felt important and threatening.

Grace looked up, again defiant. "Chuck had a lot of allergies."

I checked the level of wine in my glass. Over half full. I hadn't drunk enough that I should have lost track of the conversation, but somehow I had.

"Was the entire box filled with decongestants?" Fred understood the new topic. Apparently I was drunk after all.

Grace said nothing.

I certainly wasn't going to say anything.

"You've got to tell the police," Fred said.

"No! They'll think..." Grace's small features tightened into a fiercely protective expression. "You know what they'll think."

"I'm lost," I said. "You don't want the police to think Chuck had allergies?"

Fred and Grace looked at me as if I should be sitting in the corner wearing a dunce cap.

"Decongestants can be used to manufacture methamphetamine," Fred said.

"I know that. I watched Breaking Bad." I rebooted my brain. "Oh! You mean Chuck...?" Duh. "He knew George's friend."

"That doesn't mean anything," Grace said.

"Actually, it probably does." I was speaking more to myself than to Grace, astonished I'd missed the connection. "George just got out of prison for selling drugs. He hasn't had time to make new friends, so all those guys at the party were probably druggies too."

"You don't know that."

"I know Gaylord offered Chuck a joint."

"A little marijuana. Pretty soon it'll be legal everywhere. You shouldn't go around saying things like that. You'll make it sound like Chuck was a bad person."

"You don't think being married to half the women in the Midwest makes him sound like a bad person?"

She burst into tears.

Way to go, Lindsay! "I'm sorry! I didn't mean it that way." What other way could I possibly have meant it?

Fred produced a tissue and Grace wiped her eyes. "It's all so awful. Not bad enough my husband's dead, but he had those other wives, and the police think I killed him, and now you accuse him of cooking meth. He was a good man!"

Reminded me of Cathy Murray's assertions that her grandson, George, was a good man. Optimism? Self-delusion?

I turned to Fred. "How big was the box of decongestants George took away?"

"Average size moving box."

"How full was that box, Grace?"

70

She focused on her glass of wine.

"Even if it was only half full, that's a lot of decongestants."

"Chuck had awful—"

"I know," I interrupted. "He had a lot of allergies. Wrong answer." I leaned toward her. "Grace, you're under suspicion for murder. If Chuck was involved with drug dealers, the police need to know. That's a dangerous occupation. One of those people could have killed him. That guy who grabbed Chuck when you two were leaving was the same one who offered him a joint. What did he want? He didn't seem friendly. I thought they were going to get into a fight."

"The goofy looking guy?"

"Yes," I said. "George introduced him as Gaylord Dumford."

"He's just somebody Chuck works with. I reckon even men who smoke pot have jobs."

"What did he want?" I asked again.

"Something about a tractor that didn't get delivered on time."

"Did you hear that from him or did Chuck tell you?"

"Chuck sent me home while he talked to the guy. But Chuck said that was what happened, and he would never lie to me." Grace hesitated and gulped. "I mean..." She ducked her head and took a long drink of wine.

"In other words, we have no way of knowing what Gaylord and Chuck talked about." I applauded myself for being so tactful, not pointing out the number of things we already knew Chuck had lied to her about. "If Gaylord was alone with Chuck while you went on to the house, he could have given him something with cyanide in it."

Grace's head lifted. "Why would he do that?"

"You mentioned Chuck had lots of cash," Fred said. "Where did he keep his cash?"

"It's safe. The cops didn't find it."

"The cops didn't find it?" I repeated. "You mean it's in your house?"

Grace said nothing.

I looked at Fred. He didn't appear surprised.

But he never does.

"If someone killed your husband over drug money," Fred said, "and that drug money is in your house, you could be in danger. That could be what George was looking for."

"He wasn't looking for anything. He was just trying to help."

"By taking away all Chuck's decongestants?" I asked. "How did he know about them?"

"He found them while he was helping me unpack. He said it wouldn't look good if the cops found them so he took them away for me."

I bit my tongue and told myself to be nice. But nobody tells me what to do, not even me. "Grace, stop that. You're being deliberately obtuse. You know exactly what all those decongestants meant, where all that cash came from, and why George was so eager to help you. You could be in danger. You've got to tell the cops."

Grace's chin tilted upward and her lips firmed.

I recognized that look. I'd seen it in the mirror. No way was she going to tell the cops anything.

"If you don't tell them, I will," I said.

"If you do, you're no friend of mine."

Yesterday I hadn't been a friend of hers anyway, but her comment made me feel guilty. "You can't put yourself in danger and risk going to prison to save Chuck's reputation."

"I reckon I can if I want to. This is my secret, and you better not tell."

I squirmed uncomfortably. "I don't keep secrets well."

"Promise me you won't tell the cops," she insisted. "Not Trent, not any of them."

I looked at Fred for help. He offered none.

"Promise," she demanded.

"All right, all right!" I said.

Grace smiled. "Thank you. You're a true friend."

There's an old saying: Two people can keep a secret if neither of them is Lindsay.

Chapter Seven

Grace left with Chuck's cell phone.

I closed the door behind her and returned to my chair. "She's going to have Rickie erase all the data on her cell phone anyway."

Fred nodded. "She's in deep denial."

"That's one way to put it."

"Perhaps I'll have some of that wine after all," he said.

Grace must be in big trouble if Fred was so stressed he was willing to drink my wine.

I brought him a half-full glass. "Drink that and you can have some more."

He eyed the pink liquid askance. "Is that a promise or a threat?"

Fred's such a kidder.

I resumed my seat.

He took a drink of wine, made a face, and took another. "Grace is her own worst enemy."

"Maybe, but it's because she's trying to salvage something of her marriage."

Fred grimaced, not from the wine this time. "He had at least seven wives, and evidence suggests he was involved in the production of meth to support those wives. What's left to salvage from that scenario?"

"You don't understand."

He straightened his glasses which were not askew to begin with. "No, I don't. Explain it to me."

"Grace hasn't had a lot of luck with love."

He waited.

"Chuck was good to her. She loved him. She needs to believe that he loved her."

"He was already married to at least six women when he promised to love, honor, and cherish her, forsaking all others."

"She needs to believe he meant those words, that he'd found his true love in her, that the other women were part of his past, that he was going to forsake them."

Fred considered the idea for a moment. "That's possible but unlikely."

"I know that, and Grace probably knows it on some level, but she's going through a tough time. We are going to let her believe he might have divorced those other women and lived happily ever after with her."

Deep lines creased Fred's forehead.

"You keep frowning like that, you'll get wrinkles," I warned.

"Why do you care what Grace needs to believe? You don't like her."

I repositioned myself in my chair. Maybe I squirmed a little. "I don't dislike her."

Fred arched a skeptical eyebrow.

"Anymore," I added.

"What's changed?"

"Damn, Fred, her husband was murdered right in front of her! Don't you have any compassion?"

"Yes, of course, but she's putting herself in danger by refusing to accept reality. She's getting involved with George Murray, a known felon who may have had a part in her husband's murder, and she's hiding cash which is almost certainly drug money and which the other drug dealers are probably aware of."

"I know! And on top of all that, the cops think she killed Chuck. We have to help her."

"All right. Convince her to leave the data on Chuck's cell phone alone and tell the police everything, including the information about the decongestants and Chuck's cash business."

"Getting a divorce from Rickhead was easy compared to convincing Grace to sell out the love of her life. I have an idea. Why don't you tell the cops? She didn't make you promise not to."

"I already told them all I know, that Grace and Chuck came to your party, dropped off Rickie, and left."

"Did you tell them about Gaylord offering Chuck a joint? That would clue them in to the drug thing."

"It would also clue them in that people had illegal drugs on your property. Under the circumstances, I thought it prudent to follow your logic that it's not always necessary to tell everything we know, and neglecting to mention something is not the same as lying."

Fred applied my teachings. It didn't help Grace, but it was extremely flattering. "Can I get you some brownies?"

"Yes, please, in a to-go bag. I need to leave. You'll want to contact Trent and find out about the events of the day. It might be an opportunity to tell him Grace's secrets."

I flinched. "You know I can't do that. She made me promise not to tell Trent."

Fred left me with a dilemma. Tell Trent the information Grace was withholding in an effort to protect her or be a loyal neighbor/friend and keep her secrets even though that could put her in danger?

I set my phone on the lamp table next to my chair and left it there while I melted cheese over corn chips, added jalapenos, and called it dinner. My stomach was too knotted for real food. Besides, neither Fred nor Paula had invited me to dinner so the option of real food was off the table.

I poured the rest of my glass of wine down the sink. I blab enough when I'm sober.

Darkness settled outside my windows. I didn't turn on any lights. It's easier to keep a secret when it's dark.

I made that up, but I was ready to try anything.

Henry came home. I gave him food and catnip. As if he could sense my troubled thoughts, he settled on my lap and purred.

Maybe his compassionate gesture was due more to the catnip than feline sympathy. Whatever. I'd take it.

The evening wore on and Trent didn't call. Maybe he wasn't going to call. We talk almost every night, but almost every isn't the same thing as every. He was busy with the murder across the street. He had things to do, people to arrest. I could only hope those people didn't include Grace.

I sat in my recliner in my dark living room, watching my dark phone and hoping my boyfriend wouldn't call.

Even I realized how weird it was to hope Trent wouldn't call.

Henry would have realized it too if he hadn't been stoned.

My phone lit up and vibrated.

Text message.

Notification that my wireless bill was due.

Never thought I'd be glad to see one of those irritating messages.

It was time for me to go to bed. I had to get up early. Millions of people count on me to produce their breakfast chocolate so they can keep the world running.

Maybe it's closer to forty or fifty people instead of millions, but they all matter.

I continued to sit.

Light and music exploded from my phone.

I jumped.

Henry leapt off my lap and fled upstairs.

Left me alone to face the music, Out of a Blue Clear Sky, Trent's ring tone.

I answered. "Hey."

"Hey, you. How was your day?"

"Good. Henry didn't bring home a mouse, I gave him catnip, Fred came over, I had nachos for dinner." I was babbling, trying to talk about anything except Grace. "What did you have for dinner?" Oh, good grief! Could I come up with anything more insipid? "It's been humid today. My hair's really frizzy." Yes! I'd done it! Spoken words more insipid than I realized possible.

I decided to shut up for a while.

"I had tacos for dinner, and I like your hair when it's frizzy. Are you okay?"

"I'm fine. Grace didn't kill her husband." At least I hadn't blurted out any secrets.

"You know I can't talk about an ongoing investigation."

"That's good! I mean, I know. That's okay. I understand."

"You do?" He sounded surprised.

"Of course I do. So, what do you think about the chances of the Chiefs going to the Superbowl?" I know how to divert a man's attention. Talk about football.

Trent was silent for a long moment.

Had I gotten it wrong again? Did the baseball team go to the Superbowl?

"It's not football season," he said.

"I meant the Royals."

"It's not baseball season."

"You're kidding. I thought it was always football or baseball season and sometimes both at the same time."

"Basketball. Are you sure you're okay?"

"I'm fine. Just tired. Oh, look at the time! How did it get to be so late?"

"Yeah, I'm sorry I didn't call earlier. I had a lot of paperwork to finish. Go to bed. We'll talk tomorrow. Love you."

"Love you too."

I disconnected the call and flopped back in the chair, my heart pounding. The conversation had been excruciating, and that was bad wrong. Talking to the man I loved should make me happy. Usually it did. I couldn't betray Grace, but not betraying her felt as if I was betraying Trent.

᪜᪜

The next day at work I filled Paula in on the events of the previous evening. She wasn't associated with the cops, so I figured it was okay to talk to her about Grace's dilemma.

She slid a pan of cinnamon rolls into the oven and turned to me. "You did the right thing, keeping Grace's secrets."

I don't know what I wanted her to say, but that wasn't it. I cracked an egg. Actually, I shattered it. Barely got it into the mixing bowl instead of on the floor. "I'm going to talk to Grace and let her know I can't keep secrets like that from Trent."

"You call it keeping secrets. I call it minding your own business, staying out of Grace's predicament. You don't need to get into the middle of a murder investigation."

I refrained from bringing up the story of what happened with her ex. Yes, my meddling almost got me killed, but, if not for my meddling, she might be in prison now while her crazy ex raised Zach.

Breakfast was busy. I performed my life purpose of providing chocolate to people to make them happy. It's a fulfilling occupation.

I was in the middle of making Chocolate Ganache Cake for lunch when my cell phone rang.

I didn't recognize the number.

Damned telemarketers. I should ignore it and keep working.

I shoved the cake into the oven and set the timer. My already-frayed nerves took over. I grabbed the

80

phone to take out my irritation on somebody wanting to upgrade my credit card, sell me a vacation cruise, or tell me I owed money to the IRS. "FBI Department of Fraud. How may I direct your call?"

A moment of silence.

Got 'em!

"Lindsay?" A trembling female voice.

"Who's calling?"

"It's me, Grace. They arrested me for Chuck's murder!"

"What? How can they do that? You should have told them about the decongestants!"

"It wouldn't matter! They found cyanide in his gum and cyanide in one of the boxes at my house," she wailed. "What am I going to do?"

I looked over at Paula. She was chopping celery for chicken salad and pretending not to listen.

I had to get involved. I had to meddle.

"You need a lawyer who can get you out on bail."

"I don't know any lawyers!"

"It'll be okay. My dad's a lawyer." I was offering her false words of comfort. My dad could direct Grace to a real estate or probate attorney or some other kind that would do her no good whatsoever.

Or I could call Fred.

"It's going to be okay," I said again, and that time I meant it. "We'll get you free on bail, then we'll sort this out."

"Thank you! Can you check on Rickie? The police called Rick but he was busy. He said he'd come get him tonight so they let Fred take him before they hauled me away in handcuffs. Fred was the only

person I could think of. You and Sophie were at work."
She gulped back a sob.

Fred already knew.

And he hadn't bothered to call me.

"I can't get to Fred's house until after work, but
I'll call him. If Rickie's with him, he's fine." I don't
know if Fred uses mind control, hypnosis, or terror
tactics, but when Rickie's around him, he acts like a
human. Rickie, not Fred. I'm not sure Fred ever acts
like a human.

"Grace is in jail," I told Paula while I waited for
Fred to answer my call.

She glanced over her shoulder briefly then went
back to work. Paula isn't easily fazed.

Fred answered.

"You need to get Grace out of jail."

"I'm aware of that. By default of being the only
neighbor at home this morning, I've become the
designated babysitter for Rickie until your ex gets here
to take him which will probably be never. This gives
me significant motivation for getting Grace out of
jail."

"Have you chained the kid in the basement?"

"Those chains are rusty. He'd be able to break
them. Currently Rickie is sitting in a chair in my office,
drinking Coke and playing Internet games on his
laptop."

I gasped. "Did you give him the password to your
Internet?"

"Of course not. Nor did I give him yours. Sophie
let him use hers yesterday, and it's accessible from
here. I'm going to have to talk to her about computer
safety."

"Wait, you know my password?"

"A lot of people use their pet's name. It's not very secure."

"We'll talk about that later. In the meantime, can you get Grace out on bail or do we have to break her out?" I was only half kidding. Who knows what Fred's going to come up with? A jail break wouldn't surprise me. I could drive the getaway car.

"I'm working on it. We have to get the judge to set bail first. Since she has no convictions on her record, it shouldn't be a major problem. However, she is accused of first degree murder. I'll take care of the bail situation but she's going to need an attorney."

"You told me you passed the bar exams in Missouri, Kansas, and Oklahoma."

"I'm not up to date on criminal law. Grace needs someone who is."

I sighed. "Get Grace out of jail and we'll find her an attorney. How hard can it be? She's innocent."

"They have some compelling evidence."

"Yeah, yeah, I know. She said they found cyanide in her house and cyanide in his gum. Big deal. Chuck was into drugs. I've heard they use poisons in making meth. That's probably one of them. Howdy Doody could have given Chuck the poisoned gum when they were talking."

"It's not inconceivable that cyanide could be involved in the methamphetamine process, but at one time Grace worked for a metal plating shop in Crappie Creek which means she had access to cyanide. She also had access to Chuck's gum. The pack in his pocket had two sticks left. Both had been dusted with cyanide then rewrapped."

Chuck had taken out a stick of gum while he was in my back yard.

Had I watched him ingest the poison that killed him? Grace had beamed up at him, pleased that he was chewing gum instead of smoking.

Or was the reason she seemed so pleased with his action something darker?

Did she know the gum would be his death?

No! She was grief-stricken. Her emotion was honest.

"Grace didn't do it," I said.

"The only fingerprints they found on the gum package were hers and Chuck's."

"Whose side are you on? She was his wife! She could have handed him that package of gum when he was getting dressed or something. The real murderer wiped his or her fingerprints off the package."

"That's possible."

At least he didn't add *but unlikely.* "Priority is getting Grace out of jail, then we'll prove she's innocent."

"Check with me when you get home. I'm working on a possibility of finding some answers."

"What?"

He hung up.

I could spend the rest of the day wondering about that possibility, but that would be pointless. I could never come up with scenarios as bizarre as Fred does.

My time would be better spent figuring out who killed Chuck.

If Chuck had chewed the lethal piece of gum in my yard, it had been before he and Howdy Doody talked privately.

But that wasn't necessarily the lethal piece of gum. And the goofy-looking man could have given him the package of gum long before either of them made it to my yard.

Was I reaching, wanting George's friend to be guilty so Grace would be innocent?

❧

I arrived home that afternoon to a scene from The Walking Dead.

The five women didn't have rotting skin and weren't dragging their feet, but they were circling each other and snarling as they paced in front of Grace's house.

The tallest woman in the group strode up to the door, banged and shouted a few times, then rejoined the others.

This had to be Fred's doing.

Chapter Eight

I pulled into my driveway, all the way up to the garage, then studied the women across the street from the safety of my car. They appeared consumed with attacking each other and paid no attention to me.

Nevertheless, when I got out I closed my car door quietly and moved toward my house in a fast walk. I resisted the urge to run, didn't want them to sense fear and attack.

Henry greeted me at the front door and grumbled as he wove around my legs. It was hard to say if he was grumbling because of the women across the street or because he wanted food. I gave him food.

My phone played Wild Bull Rider. Fred.

"Are you responsible for those women at Grace's house?" I asked.

"Come to my back door. Bring a dozen cookies."

He hung up.

A dozen cookies? Either Fred was having severe chocolate withdrawal or he planned to use my cookies to soothe the savage beasts across the street.

I wasn't sure if even chocolate could calm those women.

I checked my bag of leftovers from the shop. Fred would have to make do with five chocolate chip cookies and six brownies.

Henry darted past me to the back door.

I opened it. "Don't go out front. There are zombies across the street."

He gave me an indignant glance then strolled outside.

"I know you can handle them. Just don't go home with any of them." He had, after all, run away from his former home or pet store or cat orphanage to live with me. "I have catnip!" I called after him. That should assure his allegiance.

I took my chocolate to Fred's.

He was waiting when I arrived.

I handed him the bag. "Five cookies, six brownies."

"That will work."

"Who are those women in Grace's yard?"

"More of Chuck's wives."

I followed him to the living room.

Two glasses of red wine sat on the coffee table with an open laptop between them.

He put the bag of chocolate on the table and turned the laptop to face me. "Have a seat. I turned off the sound so we can talk while we watch. Much of their conversation hasn't been audible anyway. They all tend to shout at once."

I picked up a glass and sat on the sofa. The laptop showed the women in Grace's yard. "You set up a camera."

It wasn't a question, and he didn't reply.

The quality of the video was excellent. I watched, a little frightened and a lot fascinated. "How did you get them all here?"

"I phoned them this morning. The authorities had already informed them of Chuck's death, of course. I told each one she should be at the scene of Chuck's murder at five this afternoon to discuss which wife is entitled to collect his life insurance."

I looked at my watch. "So they've been over there for half an hour?"

"Some arrived early."

"And nobody's killed anybody yet? I would think meeting your husband's other wives could cause some animosity."

"That's what I'm counting on. I wanted them to have time and opportunity to get past the grieving stage and become very angry with Chuck. When we talk to them, I want each to try to outdo the other telling us Chuck's secrets."

I shuddered as I watched the agitated women. "I think you've accomplished your goal."

"Let me give you a list of the players." He tilted his glass toward the screen. "The tall one with short, curly, blond hair, a sharp nose and pinched lips is Chaille from Hutchinson, Kansas. She pronounces her name Shelly, but she spells it C-h-a-i-l-l-e."

It was the woman I'd seen run up and knock on the door. "That's...interesting." Interesting, weird...they have kind of the same meaning.

"Other than Stella and Chaille, Chuck favored short women. The one with light brown hair and glasses is Kristi from Newton, Iowa. Alinn from Leavenworth, Kansas, has a scrunched up, simian face and a bowl haircut."

Easily identifiable. "Alinn? That's another strange name." For a strange woman.

"I'm just reporting on Chuck's wives. I can't explain his taste. Unless we find more wives, Alinn is the original Mrs. Chuck Mayfield."

"So she's entitled to the life insurance? Unless you find more wives, of course."

"There's no life insurance."

"You lied."

"Yes. The skinny one with long blond hair that looks like it's been bleached twenty times too many is Becky from McAlester, Oklahoma. The blond who looks a little like the Wicked Witch of the West except her skin's not quite as green is Anita from Lincoln, Nebraska."

No wonder Chuck married Grace. Compared to the others, she was dignified and beautiful. I could easily believe she was the love of his life.

Speaking of Grace...

"Grace can't come home to this! What were you thinking?"

"Her bail won't be set until tomorrow. These women will be long gone by then."

"Tomorrow? You couldn't get her bail set until tomorrow? That's not like you, Fred."

"She's safer in jail right now."

"Safer in jail?"

"George was searching your basement for drug money. He conned his way into Grace's house and was going through the boxes when you caught him. If he knows about the cash Grace claims is hidden in her house, it's possible others know. Our city jail is a decent place, as jails go."

"So while Grace is spending the night in the luxurious Pleasant Grove jail, where is her son? If he's still here, you must have drugged him. I don't hear any noises."

"Rick picked him up an hour ago."

I shuddered. "I'm not sure which one to feel sorry for."

"Both. Are you ready to talk to the wives?"

"Yeah, I guess so. Why isn't Stella here? She's one of the wives-in-law."

"We'll talk to Stella at another time. She knows who we are. Anonymity is essential for this meeting."

I looked at the chaos on the laptop. "Have you ever hit a woman?"

He recoiled. "Certainly not."

"So if one of them attacks me, I'm on my own?"

"They're not going to attack you."

I rubbed my jaw which still hurt from Stella's punch. "They might."

"If someone attacks you, I promise to restrain her."

"But someone will have to attack me before you restrain her?"

"I believe that's the way it works."

I rubbed my jaw again.

He looked at the laptop, at the women pacing, snarling, gesticulating. "You know how you've been talking about wanting a gun?"

"Yes."

"I have a gift for you."

I watched in astonishment as he went upstairs.

Had Fred got me a gun?

Wow! Would it be an automatic like Trent carried or a revolver like Dirty Harry used? I'd be happy with either one, but revolvers were prettier.

I studied the images of the women on the laptop.

I wouldn't shoot them unless I had to, but the mere appearance of a gun would be intimidating. I could just aim it at them and threaten to shoot.

I lifted my arm, made a finger gun, and squinted down the imaginary sights of my index finger.

"What are you doing?" Fred had returned.

I clasped my hands over my head. "Stretching."

He handed me a purple rectangular object a little thicker than a cell phone. "I don't anticipate you'll have to use this, but if you feel the need, press that button and hold it against your attacker for a couple of seconds."

I turned it over, looking at it from all angles. A loop of thin black cord dangled from one end, and two small pieces of metal decorated the other. I pressed the button Fred had pointed out.

Electricity sizzled between the two pieces of metal. I yelped and dropped the thing. "What is that?"

"It's a stun gun." He retrieved it and handed it to me again. "I got it in your favorite color."

I forced the corners of my mouth upward and tried to look appreciative. "Thank you?"

"Slip the lanyard around your wrist. If someone takes it away from you and tries to use it against you, the pin holding the lanyard slips out and disables the gun."

The gun?

"It's only a million volts," he said, "but it will disable an attacker briefly without doing permanent damage."

A million volts?

"You have to actually touch someone with the metal points for it to shock them, but, as you've seen, the display itself is intimidating. If someone advances toward you, simply press the button. She'll back down."

I asked for a gun and got a purple plastic rectangle?

"Are you ready now?"

I slid my hand through the loop, held the purple thing in my palm, and nodded.

Does a nod count as a lie?

He handed me the bag of chocolate goodies. "Take this with you. On the front porch you'll find seven folding chairs. While I retrieve the wives, please set up the five wooden chairs with their backs toward the house and the two canvas chairs against the rail facing the other chairs."

"You're bringing those women over here?"

"Of course. We can't talk to them at Grace's house."

Of course.

Chapter Nine

While Fred walked down the street to Grace's house, I set up the chairs—five wooden, one red canvas, and one purple canvas. I put the red and purple chairs against the outside rail, facing the other chairs. Fred could have the red and I'd take the purple since it matched my plastic rectangle.

That task completed, I watched Fred interact with the women. Grace's house, two doors down and across the street, was too far for me to hear what he was telling them, but they stopped fighting.

A pied piper with an invisible pipe, he led them down the street and up his front porch steps.

"Lindsay, meet Kristi, Chaille, Anita, Becky, and Alinn. Someone played a cruel joke on them, luring them to an empty house."

"Oh, my, why would anyone do a dastardly thing like that?" I tried to sound sincere.

"They all have long drives ahead of them to get home tonight, so I invited them to join us for a cold drink before they depart." Fred opened the lid of the chest to reveal bottles of water and cans of Coke nestled in ice. "Please help yourselves. The day has become quite warm, and you ladies have been out in the heat. You shouldn't get dehydrated."

The women grabbed drinks and settled in the chairs.

Anita plopped her skinny witch butt in my purple chair.

I waited for Fred to make her get out of my chair.

He selected a bottle of water then sat in the red chair without acknowledging Anita's appropriation of my purple one.

I glared at her. She was too busy stroking Fred's arm and batting her gunky black eyelashes at him to notice.

I selected a Coke and took a seat between Pinched Lips and Simian Face. Chaille and Alinn. The former smelled of discount perfume, the latter of perspiration. I tucked my shoulders in tightly to avoid touching either of them, but that had no effect on my sense of smell. Why hadn't I set the chairs farther apart?

Fred sipped from his bottle of water, crossed his legs, and leaned back. He wasn't encouraging Anita's attentions but he wasn't shoving her away either. As Sophie's friend, if this went on much longer, I'd have to zap Anita with my purple stun gun. Accidentally, of course. Stand, trip, reflexively press the button and grab her arm in an attempt to stop my fall.

"Lindsay, do you remember that man who died Saturday in the house down the street where these ladies were congregated?" Fred asked.

"Yes?" I was pretty sure that was the right answer though sometimes Fred goes down convoluted side roads.

"You're not going to believe this," he said, "but all these ladies were married to him."

I took a long pull on my Coke.

Kristi saved me from coming up with a response. "I was first," she said in a flat, nasal voice.

Alinn thrust out her chin. "No, you weren't. I was."

Chaille leaned around me to snarl at Alinn. "I was last. He left all of you to marry me."

I clutched my purple rectangle more tightly. If the two of them started fighting with me in the middle, I'd push that button and keep pushing until they dropped to the porch, immobilized by a million volts each.

"Grace married him in August," I said.

Suddenly I had everyone's attention.

"Is that the bitch who killed him?" Alinn asked.

"Allegedly killed him," Fred corrected. "The police arrested her based on circumstantial evidence. But who could blame her if she did? He lied to her. Cheated on her. Oldest motives in the world."

Silence wrapped around our little group. I could almost hear the wheels creaking in the brains of the other lied-to, cheated-on women.

Anita stopped touching Fred and sat stiffly upright, her thin lips a hard, red line. "He lied to us."

"Cheated on us." Becky's timid voice held a sharp edge.

"Have the authorities questioned any of you yet?" he asked.

"The authorities?" Chaille repeated.

"The cops," I translated.

"Why would they question us?" Anita asked.

"You have the same motives his latest wife had," I said.

"But they've already arrested her," Alinn protested. "She's guilty. Why would they come after us?"

"She has a very good lawyer," Fred said. "He'll get the charges dropped before the case ever goes to trial."

She does?

He will?

Either Fred had contacted that very good lawyer on his way to fetch the women, or he was lying.

"I'm sure you all have nothing to worry about," he continued. "I believe there's some suspicion that Chuck was involved in illegal drugs. Perhaps the authorities will focus in that direction."

Kristi's low forehead dropped lower. "Drugs?"

"He smoked." Chaille's lips pinched more tightly.

"He stopped a few weeks ago." Deep lines around Anita's mouth suggested she'd done her share of smoking. Was she angry because she didn't have anybody to join her in an after-dinner smoke? Had he tried to get her to quit too? Surely she didn't murder him because he stopped smoking and nagged at her to quit. Her brown eyes glittered with such malice, I couldn't discount the idea.

"Did he buy a lot of decongestants?" Fred asked.

"He had allergies," Kristi said. "The dumb government wouldn't let him buy enough so I had to get some for him."

"Me too," Becky said. "Every time he came home, I went to the drugstore and bought decongestants for him."

I could feel the anger sizzling through the air on Fred's porch as the women looked at each other.

"Yeah, me too," Chaille mumbled.

"Oh, my," Fred said.

Oh, my? Fred wasn't an Oh, my kind of guy.

96

"Are you saying he used you to buy products to make illegal drugs?" Fred asked incredulously. "That's despicable."

"It certainly is," I agreed.

The eyes of the wives-in-law narrowed as they scanned each other.

"He deserved what he got," Anita said.

Slowly the other women nodded their agreement.

Fred rubbed the back of his neck. "Unbelievable. He must have been a master of deception to fool all of you."

Alinn grunted. "He always brought me gifts. Every time he came home, he brought me a bird."

"A bird?" Becky asked.

"Not a real one," Alinn said disdainfully. "I collect statues of birds."

Becky leaned forward in her seat. "He brought me a bird once. I don't collect birds. I collect frogs. I guess he got us confused."

"Cats," Kristi said. "We couldn't have a real cat because of his allergies, so he brought me little cats when he went out of town except one time he brought me a wolf."

"I collect wolves." Anita looked like a fierce wolf as she spoke.

"Mushrooms." Chaille spat out the word. I had a feeling she'd destroy all those mushrooms when she got home.

"Wait till I tell Brother Daniels," Becky said. "He's our preacher. Every time Chuck was in town, we always went to church. He even met with Brother Daniels for Bible study on Thursday evenings.

Everybody in the congregation is going to be shocked."

"Chuck was a deacon in our church." Kristi looked murderous enough to have killed him. "Reverend Ward always said he was such a good man."

Anita cast her malevolent gaze on the others. "That jerk might only be at home for a few days but he always managed to find time to see Father Donovan. Didn't have time to take his wife on vacation, but he was always yammering on about doing the right thing and helping the poor."

"Same here," Chaille agreed. "Time for everybody except his wife. We didn't even get to go on a honeymoon."

"Neither did we," Kristi said.

At least Grace had a honeymoon. They'd spent it in a fishing cabin at a lake, but it was more than some of his wives had. I made a mental note to tell her when she got out of jail. It might make her feel better.

"He wanted kids really bad," Becky said. "I'm glad we didn't have any."

"Me too," Anita agreed. "His kid might have grown into an evil man like his daddy."

The group went silent. Didn't want to talk about kids?

"Lindsay, why don't you share some of your wonderful desserts with these ladies?" Fred suggested. "Lindsay makes the best chocolate desserts in the country."

"In the world." I took the box of cookies and brownies from my bag and passed it to Chaille.

"I have not eaten chocolate desserts in every country in the world," Fred said, "but I think Lindsay is very likely correct."

Chaille took a cookie and offered the box to Becky who turned up her nose and gave the box to Kristi. She picked out a brownie, got up and brought the box to Alinn who also turned up her nose.

Two of them didn't want my desserts? What kind of women had Chuck married?

Kristi gave the box to Anita. She might be a witch, but at least she took a cookie.

"What kind of relationship did you have with your in-laws?" Fred asked. "Didn't they find it unusual that he had a different wife at Christmas than the one he'd had at Thanksgiving?"

The women studied each other, their eyes sliding from side to side, calculating.

"He didn't talk to his folks," Becky said.

Chaille shifted in her chair. "He hadn't talked to them in years."

"He's an only child," Alinn said. "They put their hopes on him. Wanted him to be a doctor because they're rich and all that, but he didn't want to be a doctor."

"That's right," Anita confirmed. "He dropped out of medical school to become a salesman."

"Broke his heart them snotty rich people wouldn't have anything to do with him," Becky said.

"So Chuck's family has money?" Fred asked.

"Gas wells," Alinn said. "Lots of gas wells out in the Oklahoma Panhandle."

Again they all nodded.

He'd told the same story to each of them. Did that mean it was true or that he found it easier to keep track if he told the same lie to everybody?

"Sad when families are separated like that." Fred looked sad.

"They made sure he'd never get any of the money," Chaille said. "They put it all in trust for his kids."

His kids?

Grace said Chuck couldn't have kids because of an old football injury. Stella had said they wanted kids but never had any. Was that why Chuck had so many wives, trying to find one who'd give him a child? If he'd adopted Rickie, the kid could have been rich. That was a sobering thought. A scary thought.

I looked around at the wives. "How many kids does Chuck have?"

Nobody said anything.

I interpreted that to mean zero.

"I'm being rude," Fred said, "keeping you from your drive home. I've very much enjoyed chatting with you." He extended a hand toward the cooler. "Help yourself to a fresh drink before you leave."

They took drinks and left, driving off into the sunset.

Fred folded his arms and watched them go. "That was quite illuminating."

I mimicked his posture. "Oh, yeah."

Illuminating?

I tried to think like Fred. What had we learned?

Chuck was a thoughtful husband who brought gifts to his wives, though sometimes he got the wives confused. I could see how that might happen.

Chuck had a predilection for decongestants.

Chuck was really into church. I'd have to ask Grace about their religious preferences.

Chuck's parents were wealthy, and he'd disappointed them with his failure to become a doctor. Had he learned how to make meth in chemistry class and decided that would be a better career choice? Fewer middle of the night emergency calls?

His parents had set up a trust fund for his offspring, but none of the wives had produced any offspring except Grace who came with an instant family. Had that been part of her attraction? Or had Grace known about the trust fund and chose Chuck because of it? If she did, that was further proof she didn't kill him. She'd have waited until the adoption was final so Rickie could inherit all that money.

"If Chuck was involved in the illegal drug business—" Fred began.

"If? You think there's a possibility he wasn't?"

"We have a lot of circumstantial evidence, but at this point, we have no proof. If Chuck was involved in the illegal drug business, the question is, was his next stop a pickup or a delivery?"

"He had a lot of decongestants which would suggest he was planning to see his cook next."

"According to Grace, he also had a lot of cash. That could mean he needed to deliver that cash. Perhaps the late tractor delivery story he told Grace actually referred to a late delivery of cash."

"You think that creepy Howdy Doody guy sent George to Grace's house to find the money?"

"It's possible. However, George was trying to find money in your basement first. Perhaps he's acting on his own."

"Not like he's above stealing. He's done it before. So what's our next step? Are we going to search Grace's house to find the money or drugs or whatever? Is that the real reason you left her in jail overnight?"

"Are you suggesting we break into her home? That would be illegal."

I thought of some of the things Fred had done and began to laugh.

I sat down in the purple chair, held my head in my hands, and laughed.

Chuck had convinced seven women to marry him. Chuck attended church regularly. Chuck's family was wealthy. Chuck dropped out of medical school.

Fred had lied to five of Chuck's wives and lured them over to talk to him. Two of those wives refused my chocolate.

And Fred wouldn't break into Grace's house because it was illegal.

The world had gone completely crazy.

Chapter Ten

I tried to convince Fred I wasn't having a meltdown, but he insisted on walking me home anyway, a journey of about twenty-five feet.

Henry met us at the door, rubbed against my leg, and snubbed Fred.

Fred snubbed him back, told me to lock the door, then waited on the porch until I went inside and swore to him the door was locked.

I'd missed two phone calls from Trent. He left a message saying I didn't need to call him back if it was too late.

I took my phone to the kitchen and gave Henry some catnip.

"Trent's so trusting," I said. "Maybe I don't deserve his trust. I'm keeping things from him. More things every day. I don't think it would be a good idea to tell him about meeting the wives tonight. It's not a secret, but I think he'll sleep better if he doesn't know about them or the stun gun, don't you?"

Henry snorted. It sounded like an affirmative snort to me.

"He withholds information from me all the time. Can't talk about an ongoing investigation. Blah, blah, blah. That means I'm justified in withholding information from him. Right?"

Henry said nothing. It sounded like an affirmative silence to me.

I decided to take Trent up on his offer not to call him back if it was too late. It was definitely too late. I needed to go to bed soon. In the next hour or so.

Tomorrow I'd worry about what I could and should tell him.

When Henry woke me that morning at 3:15, the time didn't bother me. I always get up early to make chocolate while the rest of the city is still sleeping. What bothered me was that he was standing with his front paws on the window sill, looking out toward the street, yowling like a jungle cat.

I dragged myself from my warm bed into the cold darkness and went to the window. The moon had set, the street light was out again, and the darkness blended everything into shadows.

Maybe a shadow moved on Grace's front porch.

Or maybe not.

I hoped not.

"I don't see anything," I said.

Henry looked up at me with that expression of disdain cats use for creatures with inferior senses of sight, hearing, and smell.

He dropped to the floor and trotted to the bedroom door where he stood staring at the door, waiting for it to open. I was never sure if he expected it to open from his own telekinetic abilities or from an obedient human.

His obedient human opened the door.

He waited.

I sighed. I didn't want to go out. I didn't want to explore the darkness for whatever creature caused Henry's unease.

Maybe I could distract him with catnip.

I took a step into the hallway.

He shifted his gaze to my bare feet.

He was planning an outside trip and knew my feet were soft and vulnerable without enough fur to keep them warm.

I sighed again but put on a robe and my fuzzy purple slippers.

I had a small hope that I could give him enough catnip to make him forget his obsession with Grace's house. Nevertheless, I grabbed my cell phone and stun gun from the nightstand before I followed him downstairs and turned right toward the kitchen.

He turned left toward the front door.

"This way," I encouraged. "Catnip!"

He stretched up and wrapped both paws around the door knob.

"You're not going out there. I'm not going out there. What if Chuck's murderer is out there? What if some drug dealer is trying to get into Grace's house to find drugs? Worse, what if it's another wife?"

He meowed threateningly.

"Maybe we should get Fred."

He scratched at the door impatiently.

I was not the least bit impatient to go out there. "What's your hurry? It's not like we're rescuing somebody who's in danger. Grace is safe in jail, and Rickie's with his sperm donor."

He scratched again.

Grace was in jail. Her house was empty. What did Henry know that I didn't? Had some of those boxes caught on fire? My house had outdated wiring when we bought it. Grace's house probably did too. Rickhead would never bother to fix something hazardous just because it could endanger his son who would be living there.

"All right!" I opened the door.

Henry darted out and...no surprise...headed across the street at an angle, straight for Grace's house.

I wrapped my robe around me tightly. The morning was chilly. And, did I mention, dark?

I looked at Fred's house. No light shone from any of the windows. He could be awake, sitting in the darkness, doing a mind-meld with aliens.

But it probably wasn't a good idea to disturb him on the sole excuse that my cat was being weird. He and Henry don't always see blue eye to blue eye. They're too much alike. Except Fred doesn't eat mice. As far as I know.

I had my phone and my stun gun. If the house was on fire, I would call 911. If we encountered anything more than a mouse, I could stun the intruder then call Fred to help me haul off the body.

I followed Henry.

He slipped silently onto Grace's porch and planted himself in front of the door, tail waving high in the air.

He wanted to go inside.

I did not.

"Door's locked." Why was I whispering?

A light flashed inside the house.

Damn.

It was the wrong season for fireflies. Somebody was inside Grace's house.

I took my cell phone from my robe pocket and prepared to call Fred. I fumbled with the phone and almost dropped it. My hand might have been shaking a little. I'd been sort of kidding when I told Henry there could be a drug dealer, a murderer, or another wife lurking in the night.

The light flashed again, briefly illuminating a face.

My hand steadied as hot anger bubbled up from my gut and replaced the chill of the night.

George was inside Grace's house.

I didn't need Fred's help on this one. I put my phone in my pocket and took out my stun gun.

The front door swung open at my touch.

Henry darted inside.

I entered and flipped on the overhead light. "What are you doing here?"

George cursed and sprinted across the room toward the kitchen...toward the back door.

He was not going to escape so easily.

"Sic him!"

Henry and I charged.

George was on the threshold of the kitchen when I caught him, shoved my stun gun against the flannel shirt covering his back, and hit the button. He screamed, flailed his arms, and fell forward.

I screamed, flailed my arms, and almost fell backward.

My shock was mental, surprise at how effectively the plastic thing worked.

George's was physical.

He wasn't dead. He thrashed around on the floor and said some words I won't repeat.

I stood over him, holding my stun gun at the ready. "I'm going to tell your grandmother what you said!"

He cursed some more.

Henry moved closer, looked him in the eye and snarled, baring his half inch fangs.

George shut up and lay quietly.

"What are you doing here?" I asked again.

His gaze shifted from Henry to me and back again. "Grace wanted me to check on things while she's…you know…gone."

"I hate it when somebody lies to me." I zapped his knee.

He screamed and cursed and twitched some more.

This device was a good deal. With a real gun, he'd have been dead from the first shot. Torturing him was much more satisfying.

"Let's try that again. What are you doing here?"

"Go to hell, bitch!" He tried to sit up.

Henry hissed.

I zapped George's thigh. "That's bitch-with-a-stun-gun-and-a-bad-temper! Next time it's going to be your crotch."

His angry expression said a lot of evil words, but he refrained from verbalizing them.

I wouldn't have really placed my nice purple stun gun on his crotch. Who knows what disgusting creatures might leap out and contaminate my new toy?

"I'm also the bitch who's dating a cop. Maybe you'd rather talk to him so the both of you can explain to your parole officer what you're doing in Grace's house in the middle of the night."

His eyes tightened to dangerous slits.

I took a step back but kept my weapon trained on him.

With my free hand I slid my phone from my robe pocket and held it in front of my mouth. "Call Detective Adam Trent." I don't have a phone that responds to oral commands, but George didn't know that.

"No! I'll tell you!"

"It's ringing," I said. "You better talk fast."

He mumbled something.

I zapped the air. "Speak up!"

"Dumford."

"Dumford? Howdy Doody?"

"Hang up, damn it!" George shouted.

"Oh, yeah. Uh, cancel call." I returned the phone to my pocket. "What about Dumford?"

"Can you put that other thing in your pocket too?"

"No."

"Can I get up?"

"No."

George put a hand over his eyes—blocking the ceiling light or blocking my ability to see his eyes and know if he was lying? "The money Chuck stashed. I gotta find it and give it to him."

"Good grief! Not bad enough Chuck's dead, Howdy Doody wants to steal money from his widow?" One of his widows.

George was silent for a long moment. His hand still covered his eyes, but I could almost feel them shifting back and forth, searching for a reply that wouldn't get him zapped again. "It's Dumford's money. Chuck stole it from him."

"Stole it from him? Broke into his house? Robbed him at gun point?"

"Chuck sold some stuff and didn't give Dumford all the money."

Now we were drilling down to the truth. "Stuff? Drugs?"

"Let it go. You don't know who you're dealing with."

"Of course I don't know unless you tell me. But you do know who you're dealing with...a crazy bitch with a bad temper, a stun gun, and the home phone number of a cop."

George's lips...the only part of his face I could see...squeezed tighter.

Henry sat upright, his gaze fixed on something behind me.

"The lady asked you a question."

I spun around at the sound of the familiar voice.

"Fred! About time you got here." I was surprised by his sudden appearance but not surprised he was there. He'd probably been watching the entire scene on his laptop. It was courteous of him to give me time to try out my new toy before he stepped in.

"Sorry I'm late," he said. "You know how difficult it is to get blood out of white carpet."

I didn't know, and I didn't believe Fred knew either. He's much too fastidious to make a mess like that.

"The old carpet in here needs to be taken up anyway," I said.

"Not necessary. I brought a shower curtain."

George took his hands away from his face. His eyes were pools of fear. "I saw you at the party. You're the weird guy who came to see me in prison."

I grabbed Fred's arms and looked back at George. "Don't call him weird! He doesn't like to be called weird. You don't know who you're dealing with."

"It's okay," Fred said quietly. "You need to leave to get ready for work, Lindsay. I'll take care of our friend." He stepped around me, lifted one hand and let a shower curtain slowly unfold.

George scooted backward, closer to the doorframe. "No! Lindsay, you're friends with my grandma. Don't leave me." He swallowed. Actually, it was more like a gulp. "I haven't done anything wrong."

Fred shrugged. It's amazing how he can look nonchalant and deadly at the same time. "Breaking and entering, trespassing, possession of a gun when you're a convicted felon—"

"I don't have a gun!" George protested.

Interesting how Fred had so easily elicited that valuable information.

"You've got one chance to go home to your grandparents instead of back to prison."

"Yeah," I agreed. "One chance." I had no idea what that chance was.

"You need to answer Lindsay's question as to whether Chuck was selling drugs for Gaylord Dumford, then elaborate on your statement that Chuck didn't give Dumford all the money."

George squirmed into a sitting position against the side of the doorway. "I just got out of the joint. I don't know nothing."

"George, I'm a busy man. I don't have time to play games. Right now we're willing to let you walk away and pretend tonight never happened. And the key word in that sentence is walk. If you'd rather, I can carry you out of here in pieces."

George swallowed hard and looked up. "Meth," he said. "Chuck distributed meth for Dumford. He skimmed money off the top. Dumford sent me to get it back. That's all I know."

"Did Dumford kill Chuck?" Fred asked.

George's mouth opened then closed like a fish gasping for air. "I don't know nothing about murder! I just came here to find the money."

"Money Chuck stole from Gaylord Dumford?" Fred asked.

George gave a jerky nod.

"That seems a foolhardy thing for Chuck to do."

"Yeah," George agreed. "It was. It's that new woman he married. It's all her fault. She changed him. He wanted to get out of the business. You get in bed with Gaylord Dumford, you're there for life. That dude's bad crazy."

"So Chuck knew Dumford was bad crazy, but he stole money from him anyway?"

George was lying about something, but I didn't think it was the part about Dumford being bad crazy. "I'm telling you," he said, "Chuck went nuts after he married that woman. He wanted to go straight, and he had to have some money to get started on. It wasn't like he had a college degree. All he'd ever done was be Dumford's errand boy."

I made a mental note to tell Grace that Chuck had given up his life of crime for her. Maybe he really did intend to leave all those other women. That would be some solace for her while she worked in the prison laundry.

"Is that what Chuck and Dumford were talking about at the party?" I asked. "Did Howdy Doody poison Chuck because he stole money from him?"

"Maybe. I don't know. Dumford just told me he wanted to come to the party so he could talk to Chuck."

"Wait!" I said. "Howdy Doody knew Chuck would be at the party?"

"He knew Chuck was moving in across the street. He knows everything."

"You didn't invite all your friends just to distract me while you dug up my basement?"

"No!" He fidgeted and looked away. "Well, maybe, but Dumford came because he had business with Chuck. I didn't have any part of that. I just asked my grandma to do the party on that day at your house and—"

"What business did Howdy Doody have?" I asked. "A chance to murder him?"

"No. I don't know. He wanted to keep Chuck hooked. Chuck was the best. He had all those...uh...connections."

"All those wives, you mean."

George shrugged.

"I need Dumford's phone number and address," Fred said.

"I don't have it."

Fred flapped the folded shower curtain lazily. "This conversation terminates in five minutes. The method of termination is up to you."

George reached into his pants pocket.

He'd said he didn't have a gun, but George had been known to lie.

Fred didn't move.

113

I lifted my stun gun. Was I going to have to save Fred?

George withdrew his cell phone.

Fred took it from him.

"Hey!" George protested.

Fred extended the shower curtain to me. "Hold this."

I took it with the tips of my fingers even though I was certain Fred had never really wrapped bodies in it. Fairly certain. One can never be certain of anything where Fred is concerned.

"Password," he said.

"One, two, three, four," George said.

That was dumber than me using Henry's name for my Internet password.

Fred checked several things on George's phone then tossed it to him.

George caught it in both hands.

"Now get out and do not return."

"I gotta find that money. You don't get it. He'll kill me."

Fred took the shower curtain from me, rocked back on his heels, and regarded George calmly. "You need to decide who you're more frightened of, me or Gaylord Dumford."

George rose slowly to his feet. "You're getting in way over your head, man." He stumbled across the room and out the front door.

I looked up at Fred. I'm tall, but he's taller. He's even taller than Trent. How much trouble were we getting into that it would be over Fred's head?

As we walked through the living room, Fred dropped the folded shower curtain into an open box.

"Not yours?" I asked.

"I didn't think Grace would mind if I borrowed it for a good cause."

"I knew you'd never wrap a body in a shower curtain."

"Of course not. The material's too flimsy."

"Does that mean...?" I hesitated.

Fred switched off the light. "Are you going to finish your sentence?"

"Nope. Let's go. Come on, Henry."

Chapter Eleven

An hour later I staggered through the back door of Death by Chocolate, not really ready to begin my day.

Paula looked up, her knife poised halfway through slicing cinnamon roll dough. "Are you exhausted from dealing with all those women on Grace's lawn last night or does this have something to do with the lights in Grace's house early this morning?"

I found a clean apron and slipped it over my head. "Both. I need another Coke."

"Another, as in your second?"

"It's too late to start counting." I took a can from my private stock in the refrigerator and popped the top. "I don't count your cups of coffee."

"Grumpy as well as tired. You need some protein." Having delivered her sane advice, she returned to slicing the rolls.

"I'll put an extra egg in the brownies."

I gulped down a handful of nuts as I began the creation of the dessert of the day, Ding Dong Cupcakes. Thus fortified, I told Paula the details of Chuck's wives and George's break-in.

As I talked, measured cocoa powder, and breathed in the scent of cinnamon rolls baking, my tension abated.

Paula took a pan of hot rolls from the oven and set it on a rack to cool. "I saw those women in Grace's yard when I came home from work. I only met Chuck the one time, but I didn't picture him as a bigamist or being involved with drugs."

"A bigamist is married to two people. Chuck would be a septamist." I slid the cupcakes into the oven and rinsed out my mixing bowl.

"If Grace knew that, she would have a motive to kill him."

The stainless steel mixing bowl clanged when I set it on the counter. "Ever hear the phrase, innocent until proven guilty? She didn't know any of that, and she didn't kill him."

Paula said nothing.

I measured brown sugar and butter for chocolate chip cookies, my everyday special dessert. "I told you about that weird friend of George's who came to the party and offered Chuck a joint."

"The one who looked like a cartoon character?"

"A puppet, but yes, that's the one." I related my encounter with George.

Paula mixed the frosting for the cinnamon rolls. If I hadn't known her so well, I wouldn't have noticed the tension that gathered around the corners of her mouth and the jittery movements of her hands.

I finished my story.

She was silent for a moment, quietly gathering steam.

"It's only been a few months since Rick got you involved with those drug dealers," she finally said. "One was murdered in your back yard. Have you forgotten that?" She stirred the frosting with a vengeance. If that sugar hadn't been powdered when it went in the bowl, it would be now.

"No," I said. "I haven't forgotten. I eat a lot of chocolate. It has antioxidants. My memory's fine."

Paula stopped punishing the innocent frosting, looked at me, and sighed. "I'm not so sure it was a good idea for Fred to give you that stun gun. You've always been a little reckless and impulsive, but going to an empty house in the middle of the night to confront a convicted felon who broke into that house? That wasn't good judgment."

"Henry led me over there. He wouldn't lead me into anything dangerous. If anything happened to me, who'd dispense his catnip?"

I dragged out my cookie sheets, rattling them vigorously. I thumped them onto the counter, making so much noise Paula couldn't say anything rude about Henry being only a cat. She doesn't get it, that being only a cat is comparable to being only a psychic genius. I forgive her. I didn't understand that until Henry moved in and educated me.

However, plopping the dough onto the cookie sheets didn't make a lot of noise.

Paula was doing something at the far end of the kitchen with her back turned toward me. "Henry's only a cat."

"I won't tell him you said that. It might put your life in danger."

The rest of the work day moved along nicely. Nobody left without paying, nobody was rude to the server. The worst thing that happened was that we ran out of Ding Dong Cupcakes before we ran out of customers. The two people who didn't get a cupcake accepted a brownie instead, so all was well.

118

Then I left the restaurant, the place where my only responsibility was to create desserts and serve them to people who were grateful. As soon as I got home, I'd serve cat food to Henry, and he'd be grateful.

The thought that loomed over me like Edgar Allan Poe's pendulum swinging closer and closer was my upcoming evening phone call with Trent. I'd avoided talking to him last night. Two nights in a row would make him suspicious or worried or both. And now I had even more secrets. If I told him about my early morning encounter with George, I'd have to tell him about the money Grace was hiding and where that money came from.

It was possible...likely?...Chuck's choice of career had brought on his death. I was in possession of information that might exonerate Grace, might bring a murderer to justice, but she trusted me to keep that information a secret.

How far did friendship go? Was I supposed to let her rot in jail while I kept her deceased husband's secrets? Protecting Chuck's reputation to the detriment of her freedom did not seem like a good idea.

I arrived home and started across the yard to my front porch.

An old pickup truck rattled slowly down the street. We don't have a lot of traffic. Nobody I knew owned a dilapidated pickup.

But it was a public street. The driver had every right to use it. I didn't need to know everything about my neighbors and their visitors.

I curbed my curiosity, strode determinedly onto my porch, and unlocked the door.

The truck rumbled past my house.

Henry greeted me at the door and turned to lead me to his empty food bowl in the kitchen.

The rattling from the truck ended with a huff.

I looked over my shoulder.

It had stopped in front of Grace's house. I couldn't tell if it stopped because someone applied the brakes or if it simply died.

Henry came back and nudged my leg gently. Well, as gentle as a half-grown lion can nudge. I took the hint and followed him to the kitchen where I poured food into his bowl.

He dove in, crunching and purring.

Assuming the truck did not die of natural causes, who would be coming to Grace's house? Could it be another wife?

It didn't look like a vehicle a woman would drive.

But Chuck's wives were not ordinary women.

Was the truck driven by criminal cohorts of George and Howdy Doody? Were they planning to break into Grace's house in broad daylight?

Henry finished his food and went to the back door.

I let him out.

Last I heard, Grace was still in jail. Her house was unguarded. One of the terms of friendship was the protection of personal property, especially when that property included a stash of cash skimmed from drug deals by said friend's deceased husband.

It didn't sound quite so noble when I thought of it like that so I decided not to think of it like that.

I headed out the front door, cell phone in one hand and stun gun in the other.

As I passed the truck, I glanced through the open window of the cab. Nobody inside. Dingy towels that might have once been white hung over the seats and covered some of the stuffing that protruded from the worn fabric. Fast food wrappers and soft drink cups littered the floor.

I strode up Grace's sidewalk. Her front door sported two shiny new deadbolts. Fred had been there.

I stuck my phone in my pocket, held my thumb on the button of the stun gun, and grasped the door knob.

It turned.

My heart beat a little faster.

Didn't mean anything, I assured myself. The lock was old, unreliable. The new deadbolts were the main source of security.

I pushed gently.

The door moved.

Somebody was in there. Fred would not have gone away and left those locks unlocked. He was way too OCD for that.

Inside the house a woman screamed.

Another wife?

I sucked up my courage, shoved the door open, and charged inside.

Chapter Twelve

Grace stood a few feet away, eyes and mouth wide.

I stopped. My heart was racing, and my eyes and mouth were probably as wide as hers.

"Lindsay! You scared me! I thought somebody was breaking in."

I wasn't going to admit she had scared me too. "I'm sorry. I was worried. I didn't know you were out of jail."

She flushed and turned toward a grungy couple sitting on the sofa.

"Lindsay," she said, "come in and meet my in-laws."

"Your…in-laws?"

"Chuck's parents."

The wealthy folks from Oklahoma?

In that truck?

"This is Edwina and Leon Mayfield." With her bright hair pulled back in a ponytail, no makeup, and a big smile, Grace looked like a child on Christmas morning.

The couple on the sofa, not so much. I did not feel a warm welcome emanating from them.

They rose slowly to their feet.

Faded overalls hung loosely on the man's tall, lanky frame. His overgrown dark blond hair and beard could provide shelter to any number of creatures. I was glad Henry wasn't with me. He might get fleas.

The woman was short and squatty. With her shapeless brown dress and morose expression, she resembled a toad wearing a slightly askew blond wig.

"Lindsay's my neighbor and my best friend," Grace said proudly.

I'd graduated from her friend to her best friend. More responsibility. More secrets.

Leon's beard moved. Could be smiling. Could be snarling. Could be the residents having a workout. "Anybody who's a friend of our daughter is our friend."

Their daughter? Oh, puke.

I closed the door behind me. "Pleased to meet you," I lied.

Was I being unfair?

One cannot judge others by their appearance. If they lived in the country and drove regularly on dirt or gravel roads, an old truck made sense.

But Mr. Mayfield could surely afford a razor, and shouldn't Mrs. Mayfield have been able to buy a better wig? Bless her heart, maybe she didn't realize how bad it looked.

"I was just going to get drinks for everybody." Grace fluttered. "I know you want Coke, Lindsay."

"Me too." Until he spoke, I hadn't noticed Rickie huddled on the far corner of the sofa.

Mrs. Mayfield patted his head.

Rickie cringed.

For once, I was with him.

"All right, Coke for everybody!" Grace started toward the kitchen.

"Let me help you with that," I said.

"I don't need any help."

"Yes, you do." I followed her into the kitchen. "Those people out there are Chuck's wealthy parents?"

She beamed. "They want me to call them Mom and Dad."

Mom and Dad. They'd played the family card. Grace was putty in their grimy hands.

"They're not really your in-laws. I'm pretty sure your marriage to Chuck wasn't legal."

Her bright expression dimmed.

I have a knack for saying the wrong thing. It's a talent. Takes up the brain space where some people store their musical ability. "I mean, you and Chuck had a spiritual bond but that doesn't make those people out there your family."

She took five glasses from the cabinet. "They didn't know I was in jail." She kept her gaze averted from mine.

Some friend I was. I burst in the door saying the wrong thing then compounded it with my remark about her marriage not being legal. "I'm sorry. I didn't mean—it's my big mouth. Words just fall out."

She touched my arm. "It's okay."

Her ready forgiveness made me feel even more guilty.

She opened the refrigerator and filled a glass with ice.

I stopped her. "Pour the Coke in first then add the ice. Doesn't bubble over as much." Showing her how to dispense Coke the best way was small reparation for my actions, but it was something.

She opened a two-liter bottle and began pouring. "They want Rickie to call them Grandma and Grandpa." Her voice was as bubbly as the soft drink.

"What does Rickie think about that?"

"He's a sensitive boy. It's going to take him a while to get used to having grandparents."

Sensitive? Were we talking about the same Rickie? "How long is a while? They live almost five hundred miles away. They're not likely to come back to visit every other weekend."

"They're here for the funeral, and we can't have that until the police let me have Chuck back."

I had a bad feeling I knew where this was going. "Okay, so that'll be a few days, maybe a week. You think that's long enough for Rickie to accept those people?"

Grace turned her attention to adding ice to the half-full glasses of Coke. "I invited them to stay with me for as long as they want."

My bad feeling was right. I was becoming as psychic as Fred.

I bit my tongue just in time to prevent the words Are you out of your freaking mind? from spilling directly from my mouth, bypassing any seldom-used filter that might exist. "Do you think that's a good idea? You don't even know these people."

"They're family," she said firmly.

"You're not even completely unpacked yet. Do you have a guest room set up for your new family to stay in?"

She added another ice cube to one of the glasses. Plop. Fizz. "Rickie won't mind letting them use his room."

"Really? And where is he going to sleep?"

Plop. Fizz. "The sofa?" Clearly she had not thought this through.

"The sofa where Chuck died?"

She flinched. "They can have my bed, and I'll sleep on the sofa."

I placed both hands on the countertop and leaned against it. The primary purpose of that movement was to keep myself from strangling Grace, my new best friend. "Are you aware that George Murray broke into your house last night trying to find drug money? What if he comes back tonight?"

She picked up three of the glasses at once, an amazing feat considering she had small hands. She had probably been a good waitress. "When Fred bailed me out of jail, he told me all about George. He put deadbolts and chains on both my doors. We're safe."

Deadbolts and chains might protect her from George and his cronies, but they wouldn't protect her from those creepy people in her living room.

"Grace, how do you even know these people are really Chuck's parents? Howdy Doody might have sent them to get into your house and find Chuck's money. That truck doesn't look like something wealthy people would drive."

"They're not rich like fancy people. Chuck told me they were just farmers until somebody found gas on their land. Farmers drive old, beat-up trucks on the back roads because they'd ruin a new one."

"I know you want them to be family."

The corners of her eyes tilted down. She still looked like a little girl on Christmas morning but now it was a little girl who didn't get the doll she wanted, a little girl who discovered there's no Santa Claus. "I need them to be family."

"No, you don't! You have friends and you have Rickie."

"That's right. I have Rickie. Who's going to take care of him if I get sent to prison for Chuck's murder? His father?"

I opened my mouth. For once no words fell out.

"Can you get those other two drinks?" she asked.

Somehow I would have to save her and Rickie from her newly-found family. I was her best friend. She was my responsibility. I had to keep her out of prison and get rid of the Mayfields while keeping her secrets about Chuck's decongestant activity.

I picked up the glasses. "Fred's got an air mattress. I'll ask him if you can borrow it." I needed his help more than his air mattress, but it was a good excuse to get him over there.

I followed her into the living room and handed Rickie a Coke.

"Thanks." He sounded sincere. And a little desperate, as if he knew I was his only ally. I'd been wrong when I thought that things couldn't get any stranger than meeting Chuck's wives.

Grace and I sat in the chairs opposite the sofa, opposite the Mayfields.

"You must be exhausted from your drive," I said. "How long did it take you to get here?"

"Almost eight hours," Leon said. "Old truck don't go as fast as it used to. Neither do I, but we manage okay back home on the farm."

Grace gave me a triumphant look.

"Got a big farm, do you?" I asked.

127

"Big enough," Leon said.

"I'll bet it's real pretty," Grace said.

Grace had never been to the Oklahoma Panhandle.

"We think it is," Edwina said.

"Got me a nice little pond," Leon said. "Anytime I need to get my head on straight, I just go down and see Dr. Catfish." He slapped his leg and chuckled.

Edwina giggled.

Grace blinked a couple of times then joined the laughter.

I looked at Rickie. He pointed a finger gun at the side of his head and pulled the trigger.

Again we were in agreement.

I waited for the laughter to die. "What do you grow?" I asked, wondering if he'd say something cutesy like gas wells.

"Used to grow a little corn, but the dirt's as worn out as me and that truck."

I looked at Grace who was no longer looking at me. "So how do you make a living if you don't grow corn?" Yes, it was an incredibly rude question, but I needed to know the answer. Grace needed to know the answer.

Leon leaned forward and put a hand behind him. "I'm down in my back. Government sends us a little money every month, but not much. Chuck used to send us money pretty regular."

Ding! So much for the gas wells lie. Did that count as one lie for the gas wells and a second lie for the wealth? One ding or two? At this point, who was counting?

"Don't know what we'd have done without that boy," Edwina said. She dabbed at her eyes though I didn't see any moisture.

"That's got to be tough," I said, "losing your only child." I expected his parents to say he had twenty siblings.

Leon didn't disappoint. "Only child? We got eight kids."

Ding! I was off by twelve. Math was never my best subject.

"Seven," his wife corrected.

Leon's brows drew closer together. "You sure?"

Edwina counted on her fingers. "You're right," she said. "I wasn't counting Chuck. He's been gone a long time."

Leon nodded. "Yeah.

"Dropped out of medical school, did he?" I asked.

To my surprise, Leon nodded again. "Yeah."

"High school," Edwina corrected. "Leon's getting a little deaf."

"Yeah," Leon repeated. "Dropped out of school when he was...I dunno...fifteen, sixteen."

"When you got that many kids," Edwina said, "it's hard to keep up with all of them. You don't notice for a day or two when one of them's gone."

I was beginning to understand Chuck a lot better. He hadn't had a Leave it to Beaver childhood. More like Lady MacBeth meets Frankenstein.

Grace sat rigidly, her horrified gaze fixed on the couple.

Did she regret inviting them to stay with her? Surely she regretted any thoughts she'd had about them taking care of Rickie if she were sent to prison.

"How did you find out about Chuck's death?" If they weren't sure when he left home, how would they know when he died? It hadn't been long enough for them to notice the checks had stopped coming.

"Sheriff Hawkins come by and told us. We didn't even know he was married, but we got here as quick as we could to be with our daughter in her time of sorrow."

He hadn't known his son was married? Did that mean he didn't know about the other wives? How would this play out when the Mayfields realized they had six more daughters-in-law?

The cell phone tucked in the right pocket of my jeans vibrated. I ignored it. This situation was far more important than any text message. "So you came here to find your..." I swallowed and forced myself to continue. "Your daughter-in-law." That designation was bad enough. I refused to call her their daughter. "I guess you'll probably want to get back home as soon as possible to..." To what? They didn't need to plant crops anymore. They had no gas wells to guard or whatever one does with gas wells. They wouldn't be watching the mailbox for a check from Chuck to arrive. "To feed your dog?" Please don't let an innocent dog be dependent on these people for care!

Grace appeared to be in shock. I couldn't tell if she was pleased I was trying to get her out of her obligation to host these people or if she was horrified at all the revelations.

Edwina and Leon looked confused, but they sort of looked that way all the time.

Rickie fisted his hand at his side with the thumb extended upward.

"We don't have a dog," Edwina said.

"We're going to be here with our new daughter for a nice long visit." Leon leaned back on the sofa, settling in. That sofa would have to be burned when they left.

If they left.

"You got a real nice place here," Edwina said.

The house had lots of character, but I wasn't sure I'd call it real nice. Matted gold shag carpet hid the hardwood floors. The paint on the walls had probably once been white or maybe beige or yellow. Currently it had varying shades of all those colors. Perhaps Edwina could see beyond the cosmetic makeover the place needed.

Or perhaps Grace's house in its current condition was nice compared to hers.

If they thought she had a nice house, did they think she could afford to continue sending checks to them?

Was I being paranoid, taking this best-friend job too seriously?

Someone knocked on the door.

Grace shot out of her chair and raced across the room.

I was right behind her with Rickie bringing up the rear.

Grace opened the door.

"Good afternoon, Grace." Fred looked dignified in his dark blue slacks and gray blazer. Except for the absence of an ascot, he looked a lot like Professor Walter Keats, an identity he'd assumed a few months ago. "I see you have visitors, so I won't intrude. I just need to borrow Lindsay."

131

"No!" Rickie whispered.

"Fred, I'm in the middle of something important." I tilted my head backward, toward the Mayfields.

"I texted to let you know we have an appointment across town," he said. "And we need to leave now."

"We...do?"

"Yes, we do."

"Are we going to see the puppet man?"

"More or less."

That was a strange response, but Fred's strange.

"Go," Grace said.

"Stay," Rickie said.

Fred needed my help getting the truth out of Howdy Doody.

Grace needed me to get rid of her in-laws.

Howdy Doody could be the key to keeping Grace out of prison.

"I'll be back," I said.

"You don't have to." Grace didn't sound certain.

"You better be back." Rickie sounded certain.

Chapter Thirteen

"I can't believe you got that creep to agree to talk to us," I said as soon as Grace's door closed behind us. "What kind of story did you give him? Who are we going to be tonight?"

"Dumford's out for the evening. We're going to talk to his wife."

I almost fell going down the porch steps.

Fred grabbed my arm. "Are you okay?"

"He has a wife?" Yuck!

"And two daughters."

I stared at Fred in disbelief. "This man is a drug lord, but he has a wife and family?"

He urged me across the street to his 1968 white Mercedes waiting in his driveway. "Have you forgotten that Chuck had several wives and would have had a son if he'd lived a few days longer?"

"I know, but...never mind. This should be interesting. How did you get his wife to agree to talk to us?"

"I haven't spoken with Mrs. Dumford."

"Then how do you know her husband's out for the evening?"

"Technology."

Technology? Did that mean he'd spied on Howdy? Eavesdropped? Had a psychic vision? No, that last wouldn't utilize technology.

We reached his car and he opened the passenger door for me.

I got in.

He closed it…gently, firmly, quietly.

Fred's always a gentleman. I'm certain he would open and close the car door for me even if he weren't worried I'd slam it or get chocolate on the handle.

He got into the driver's seat and backed down the driveway in a completely straight line.

"If you didn't talk to his wife, how did you make an appointment for us to meet with her?"

We proceeded down the street, at all times maintaining equal distance between the curb and the white line.

"Had I asked for a meeting, she likely would have refused. It will be more difficult for her to turn us away in person."

"So we're going to show up on her front porch, unannounced, and you're going to scam her into telling us about her husband's drug business. That's the plan?"

"That's the general idea but we'll lead into it with a little more subtlety."

"How do we do that? You want me to talk to her woman to woman, offer my chocolate chip cookie recipe in exchange for her favorite meth recipe?"

"I doubt the subject will come up, but if it does, feel free to discuss cooking with her."

Fred doesn't always understand sarcasm.

"Does that mean I'm going to be Lindsay who makes chocolate for the masses?"

"Tonight you're my daughter, Carly. You're moving to town and want to get your daughter in school with the Dumfords' daughters."

I groaned. "Are you sure I want to do that to my daughter? Am I mad at her or something?"

He pulled up in front of a two-story house in an upscale neighborhood on the Kansas side. It looked like the home of a banker or a lawyer, not Howdy Doody, the drug dealer.

"It's so normal."

"Like the home of a successful insurance salesman?"

"An insurance salesman? Is he as successful a salesman as Chuck was?"

"Yes. Which, of course, begs the question as to how he can afford this house and private school for the kids. His wife doesn't work."

Together we went up the sidewalk that bisected the well-manicured lawn. Not as well-manicured as Fred's, but close. This lawn was probably cared for by a professional service whereas Fred has those elves.

"What if Howdy comes home unexpectedly while we're here? Are you packing heat?"

"Are you?"

I patted my shoulder bag which held my purple stun gun. "Yep."

We ascended the steps to the front porch and Fred pressed the doorbell.

Chimes sounded from inside the house.

A woman opened the door. "Can I help you?" Her medium-length blond hair and subdued makeup were perfect. She wore beige ankle pants and a matching blouse. She was every inch a competent, in-charge

Johnson County housewife. Every inch, but not every millimeter. Something was off. Her pale eyes held a hint of uncertainty. The silk blouse revealed a slight slump to her shoulders. An invisible air of insecurity wafted from her. I'd seen all those signs before…when I first met Paula.

Was Howdy Doody abusive? That would not surprise me.

Fred extended his hand. "You must be Laurie Dumford. Gaylord's told us all about you. I'm Henry Benton, and this is my daughter, Carly. Carly went to school with your husband, and I taught both of them history in the ninth grade."

Laurie made no move to take Fred's outstretched hand. "Henry Benton?" she repeated. "I don't believe my husband has mentioned you."

"We apologize for dropping by like this," I said. "We were in the neighborhood, and I just wanted to stop and say hi to my old friend."

Laurie didn't look at all reassured by my friendliness. "My husband can't see you right now. He's…busy."

Had Fred been wrong about Howdy's absence or was his wife lying?

Fred was never wrong. And Laurie hadn't actually said he wasn't home, just that he was busy.

"I remember Gaylord when he was a little boy," Fred said. "He came to birthday parties at our house. Carly, do you remember the year he fell out of our big old elm tree?"

"I sure do, Daddy. He cried like a baby."

Fred chuckled. Fred laughs, but he never giggles or chuckles in real life, only when he's playing a role.

"You two were barely more than babies at the time. Hard to believe you're both grown up now with families of your own."

Laurie gave a tight half-smile. She didn't appear amused at the hilarious story.

"Carly's right," Fred said. "We should have called first. My daughter was so eager to talk to you..." He started to turn away.

"To me?" Laurie took the bait.

"About the school your daughters go to. Carly heard a lot of good things about the school from a mutual friend. Now that she's moving up here from Lassiter, Arkansas, she wanted to check into it for my granddaughter."

Fred had just made himself a grandfather. He was never going to hear the end of this.

"Good old Lassiter High," I said. I'd been a nerd in school, but this was my chance to rewrite history. "I was a cheerleader. Daddy took me to every game."

Laurie studied us closely. The detail of Howdy's hometown in Arkansas seemed to reassure her slightly. "My daughters go to Messianic Resurrection. It's a good school. I highly recommend it. I'll tell my husband you came by." She took a step backward into the house.

"We were hoping you could give us a few more details about the school," Fred said. "Since Carly and her husband will be new to the area—"

"Daddy, we have to tell her the truth," I interrupted. For once, I knew more than Fred about what would hook this woman. "My husband isn't coming with me. I'm divorcing him. I need to know the details of any school I send my daughter to." I lowered my gaze and my voice. "I need to know she'll be safe."

Laurie gasped. "Did your husband hurt your daughter?"

"Not yet. Most of his anger was directed at me, but I knew it was only a matter of time." I took Fred's arm and looked up at him. "Thank goodness Daddy was able to rescue me."

He patted my hand. "I'll always take good care of my daughter and granddaughter."

Laurie licked her lips and looked up then down the street. Expecting her husband to return or checking to be sure the neighbors weren't watching her talk to strangers of dubious origin? "If you want to come in for a few minutes, I can give you some details about the school...phone numbers and who to talk to."

I clasped my hands and looked grateful. "Thank you." I felt a tiny bit guilty at scamming this woman who seemed nice. But she was married to a scumbag.

Not that I had any room to criticize. I'd been married to Rickhead.

The place had a tiled entryway, high ceilings, and a staircase off to one side. But even with several lamps, it was dark. Brown curtains covered all the windows, blocking the sunlight, keeping the outside world out and the inhabitants trapped inside. The carpet was taupe or maybe brown. Hard to tell in that light. The beige sofa matched the two chairs. The lamps matched each other. Sophie, with her decorating skills, would have choked from the excruciating boredom.

Fred and I sat on the beige sofa.

"I'll get that information and be right back." Laurie left the room.

"Howdy isn't here," I whispered. "I'd be able to smell him if he was."

Fred rolled his eyes. He does that a lot. Good exercise.

Laurie returned with a brochure and handed it to me. "This has addresses and phone numbers. It's a small, faith-based school with excellent security and students from good families. Your daughter won't be around ruffians and people like that."

Ruffians and people like...drug dealers? Who needed to go to school for that when they could find it right at home?

"You have a lovely house," Fred lied. "Gaylord's done well. I always had so much respect for him, the way he came back after his problems in high school."

Laurie blinked in confusion. "His...problems?"

Fred waved a hand in a negligent gesture. "All part of the past. He's got his own business, lovely home, lovely family."

Laurie's taut features relaxed slightly at the compliment. "Thank you."

"Where are your daughters? I was hoping we'd get to meet them."

"They're upstairs in their rooms, studying."

Fred chuckled again. "My granddaughter's a lot more rambunctious than your daughters. Zoe's ten. How old are your girls?"

"They're eight and ten."

Something told me Fred had not picked his granddaughter's age at random.

"How wonderful," he said. "Zoe will be in the same class as Gaylord's daughter. Maybe some of your daughter's manners will rub off on her."

Laurie's features relaxed another tenth of a degree. "Hannah will be a good influence." Relaxed enough she actually called her daughter by name. "It's not easy to raise children in this world. The church and the school help, and my husband has very strict rules."

Her husband still didn't have a name. Was it sacrilegious to speak his name? Or dangerous, like Voldemort?

"My estranged husband had strict rules too. If…" What the heck was my daughter's name? "If Zoe or I disobeyed, he got really mad."

Laurie looked away, toward the curtained windows. "God made man the head of the family. Someone has to make the rules or the family unit won't hold together."

She spoke the words by rote, words she'd probably memorized after hearing them repeated to her over and over.

I leaned forward. I wanted to say, God never told me that. But I had to play the game. "I don't think God meant when men are on drugs."

She gasped and took a step backward. "Did your husband take drugs?"

"Meth." I spread my hands in a helpless gesture. "Who knew when he went off to work in the morning, he was really going to a meth house? The money was good until he got addicted to his own product." Fred isn't the only one who can make up stories on the fly. I dropped my head and sighed dramatically.

"How awful. You're doing the right thing, putting your daughter into a faith-based school where she'll be safe from bad influences."

My daughter would be a bad influence.

"Absolutely," Fred agreed. "You're so lucky to have Gaylord. He doesn't even drink now, does he? He's turned his life around so well, become a good husband and father."

Laurie blinked again when Fred threw out the second reference to Dumford's checkered past. "He's a good man. He's a deacon in our church."

Déjà vu! Or, to be more precise, déjà entendre. I'd heard that from a couple of Chuck's wives.

Were these churches some weird religion that used meth to talk to God the way the hippies in the '70s used LSD?

"Your husband's a busy man," Fred continued in a phony, obsequious voice, "working at his insurance company all day, helping the church, and raising his beautiful family. I'm sure he couldn't do it without your support."

"You said my husband had problems in high school." Her voice was scarcely louder than a whisper. "What kind of problems?"

"The usual. You know how boys are at that age." He chuckled for the third time. "And girls. Carly's mother died when Carly was six so I had to raise her on my own. The teenage years can be difficult. Your girls are lucky to have a mother and a father around to guide them."

He stood.

So did I.

Were we leaving already? We hadn't learned anything.

Fred held out his hand to shake. This time Laurie took it. "On second thought, there's no need to tell your husband we came by. He might feel bad that he missed us."

She nodded slowly.

Was he hypnotizing her?

"He's not here, is he?" Fred asked.

She shook her head.

"Is he doing volunteer work at church?"

She nodded again. "He'll be back by midnight. He's always back by midnight."

Fred released her hand. "So nice to meet you, Mrs. Dumford."

We walked out into the gathering shadows and chilly air.

Neither of us spoke until we were in Fred's car.

"That was enlightening though not surprising," I said. "Figures Howdy Doody would be an abuser. What was all that about his bad boy days? Did you make that up?"

"Of course not." Fred turned the key, and the Mercedes engine purred to life. He eased the car smoothly along the street, into the dusk of evening. "Dumford was quite the party boy in Arkansas. That's why he had to leave. He had a decent job in construction, but he partied too much. Got into drugs. Gambled too much. Borrowed money from the wrong people. Eleven years ago, he moved to Kansas City, joined the church where he met Laurie, and turned his life around."

"He went from taking drugs to dealing them? What kind of turnaround is that?"

He eased around a corner on all four wheels. "I didn't say it was a good kind of turnaround, but he got his debts paid. Now he has a house, a family, and he volunteers at the church."

"It's kind of creepy that Chuck and Dumford were both church members. I don't suppose there's anything in the Bible that prohibits making or selling meth, but it seems a little wrong."

"I did think it something of a coincidence that all his wives lived in towns with a prison nearby."

What?

I wasn't going to admit I had no idea what he was talking about. "Yeah, me too."

I tried to recall the hometowns of the various wives. Stella was from Moberly, Missouri. Becky was from McAlester, Oklahoma. Anita...I couldn't remember the rest. It hadn't seemed important at the time. Kansas, Oklahoma, Iowa, and Nebraska. I could research but it would be easier to take Fred's word for it.

Besides, I had no idea where he was going with that data. The wives would be able to visit if Chuck went to prison for dealing drugs. Would he be able to get transfers from one prison to another since he had more than one wife to be close to?

Fred did not expound. He knew I was bluffing, that I had no idea what he was talking about.

"All right, I give up. What does the prison connection have to do with anything?"

"I suspect we'll find that each of the churches Chuck attended has a strong prison ministry. Quite a clever way to smuggle drugs into prisons."

Yikes.

A little blasphemous, but clever.

"You're missing one wife," I said. "There's no prison near Grace's home town, Crappie Creek."

"She and Chuck moved to Kansas City. There are quite a few detention centers around here."

"Maybe he married Grace because he loved her and he never intended to use her for his drug business."

"Maybe."

"It was nice of you to bail her out of jail today."

"She has no priors. I got her released on her own recognizance."

"You got her released on her own recognizance on a murder charge?"

"Yes."

"That's unusual." I could have said, That's unheard of, but obviously it was heard of in Fred's world.

"It depends."

I let it go. He wasn't going to reveal any secrets. Just as well. I already knew too many secrets.

We rode in silence the rest of the way home. Fred doesn't talk a lot anyway, and I was busy thinking. Being released on her own recognizance meant Grace could leave town, run away, hide, and it was unlikely any bounty hunters would track her down because there would be no money in it for them. I hoped she didn't know that. I hoped we would find the real murderer before that became necessary.

Chapter Fourteen

My house and Fred's house were dark when we pulled into his driveway.

Grace's was aglow.

That truck still sat in the street.

"We've got to help her." I tried to make the words come out as a positive statement rather than an uncertain question.

"Who?"

"Grace. Those people are going to take advantage of her."

"How?"

"I'm not positive exactly how, but I don't trust them. Maybe they expect her to send them checks like Chuck did. Maybe they think she has a lot of money."

"She doesn't so she can't send very many or very large checks. The way she's guarding whatever cash Chuck left behind, I doubt she's going to share with them anyway." He unbuckled his seatbelt.

"You don't understand. They played the family card. Grace wants a family, and they've moved in on her. They may never leave!"

"And what are we supposed to do about that?"

Fred was asking me what we were going to do? I had no idea. "Just get your air mattress and meet me over there."

"I don't want those people to sleep on my air mattress."

145

I opened my mouth to protest that his air mattress was latex, that whatever those people left on it would wash off.

But I couldn't bring myself to say it. I understood how he felt.

"We'll make sure Rickie or Grace sleeps on your mattress in the third bedroom. I just don't want either of them to sleep on the sofa where they'll be vulnerable if George or Howdy or somebody else breaks in."

"Pity the somebody who breaks in on Rickie." He sighed. "Very well. I'll bring the twin bed and meet you over there."

I crossed the street to Grace's house.

When she answered the door this time, her smile was a little less perky but still determined. "Come in. We have some pizza left."

My stomach grumbled. "That sounds good." I followed Grace to the kitchen.

Plates with pizza remnants surrounded a large cardboard box in the middle of the table.

Edwina and Leon sat at that table. "Well, lookie who's here," Leon said. "Set yourself down. We got some pizza left. Edwina, get Linda a plate and a beer."

I didn't bother correcting him about my name. I was too busy being horrified that he was usurping the role of host in Grace's home.

She sank meekly into her chair, letting him get away with it.

Edwina obediently rose and headed for the cabinet.

"I don't drink beer, and I don't need a plate." I'd eat off the floor before I'd take a plate from that woman. She had no right passing out Grace's plates.

I opened a folding chair and sat next to Rickie who was looking down as if he couldn't stand the sight of the people intruding into his world.

Actually he was looking down at the game he was playing on the cell phone in his lap.

Edwina took a plate from Grace's cabinet, ignoring me while obeying Leon.

I'd missed his coronation as king. Didn't even receive an invitation to the event.

I snagged a piece of pizza with a napkin. "No plate. I'm good."

She set the plate in front of me anyway and got a bottle of beer from the refrigerator.

Grace appeared to be okay with the situation.

I wasn't.

Rickie never looked up from his game, but his ears flamed red. He wasn't okay with the situation either.

I bit off the point of the pizza slice and shoved the beer toward Rickie. "Here, you can have this."

That got Rickie's attention...and Grace's.

"No, he can't!" She snatched the bottle away.

"Just kidding," I said.

Rickie gave me a conspiratorial grin then turned back to his cell phone.

What had the world come to when Rickie and I were co-conspirators?

"We're just trying to talk our new daughter into coming home with us for a visit," Leon said.

There was that d word again.

Grace beamed. "Rickie and I would love to see your farm. Rickie can get out in the clean air and go fishing and see where his daddy grew up."

Rickie stood abruptly and slammed his chair backward so hard it hit the wall. "I'm not going to your stupid farm, and that man was not my daddy. He was a liar and a cheat and he was married to a bunch of other women! I hate him!" Rickie shoved past me and ran out of the room.

No one spoke. No one even breathed loudly.

"What's he talking about?" Leon asked.

Grace looked at me, her Bambi eyes pleading.

Leon and Edwina followed her lead and turned to me.

The position of Grace's best friend was not an easy one to fill.

I folded my hands on the table. "Well, you see, it's kind of a long story."

A knock sounded on the front door.

I shot to my feet. "Fred's bringing an air mattress. That's probably him."

It might be George or a late night insurance salesman or even my ex, but I was grateful for whoever had interrupted.

Grace and I headed for the living room. We squeezed through the kitchen doorway together. I beat her through the living room by a solid fourteen inches and flung open the door.

Fred stood there holding a small bag. Only he could compress an air mattress back into the original bag. Magic.

"Come in," Grace and I invited at the same time.

Fred didn't move.

148

I grabbed his free arm and tugged.

He stepped inside. "I don't believe I've ever seen someone so excited about an air mattress."

I held tightly to his arm. "Come to the kitchen. You need to meet Chuck's parents."

"No, I don't. I need to leave this with you and go home." He extended the bag to Grace.

Leon emerged from the kitchen with Edwina close behind. "Who are you?" Leon demanded, as if he had the right to challenge Grace's visitors.

Fred regarded the intruder with disdain. "I'm Fred Sommers. You must be Chuck's father."

Leon hesitated. "You knew my son?"

"Not really."

"Fred's my neighbor," Grace said. "This is Leon Mayfield, Chuck's daddy."

"A pleasure to meet you," Fred lied then tried to escape out the door. I held his arm.

"You have to show us how to set up this bed," I said.

"You know how to set up this bed. You've borrowed it before."

"You know how to set up the bed, and I know how to make chocolate chip cookies." I sent him a telepathic message: And if you ever want to eat my cookies again, you will stay and help me.

He got my message.

"Grace, would you allow me to assist you in setting up this bed?" he asked.

Grace led us upstairs to the end of the hall. Boxes lined the walls of the small room leaving barely enough space for a bed.

Fred unfolded the twin size mattress on the floor then stood holding the cord to the internal pump. "We need an electrical outlet."

I waited for him to use his x-ray vision to penetrate the boxes and find that outlet.

Grace pointed to the back wall. "I think there's one on that side."

Fred, Grace, and I began moving boxes.

I set a heavy one (books? rocks? meth crystals?) off to one side and noticed Leon and Edwina standing in the doorway. "We could use some help," I said.

Leon put his hand to his lower back again. "I can't lift anything over five pounds."

"Makes it hard for him to go to the bathroom." Edwina giggled.

Leon chuckled.

I fought the urge to vomit. I could not allow these people to stay with Grace.

We found the outlet and Fred plugged in the bed. The noise of the pump made conversation impossible. Thank goodness. One more word out of Leon's mouth and I might lose control and zap it with my stun gun. Would his beard sizzle? Only one way to find out.

Too soon the bed was filled and Fred turned off the pump.

Grace pushed on the top. "Doesn't that look comfortable? I'll just get some bedding and be right back." She left Fred and me alone with those people.

"What did the kid mean about Chuck being married to other women?" Leon asked.

Fred shrugged. "You know how kids are."

"Yeah, I reckon we do."

"You folks plan to be in town long?" Fred's folksy accent was new.

"We want to get to know our new daughter and grandson," Leon said.

"You have three daughters, four sons, two daughters-in-law, three sons-in-law, and twelve grandchildren already," Fred said. "It's really nice of you to spend so much time with Grace and Rickie."

I could almost hear the rusty wheels trying to turn in Leon's brain so he could figure out how to respond to Fred's comment.

"They're all we have left of Chuck," Edwina said.

Interesting comment from someone who hadn't noticed her son missing for a day or two.

"Here we are!" Grace appeared with sheets, pillow, and blanket. "Let's go back to the living room where we can sit down." She tossed her load onto the bed. "I'll make this up later. I'll sleep in here tonight, and you all can have my room."

Edwina walked over and hugged Grace. "You are just the sweetest daughter we've ever had."

Gag.

Someone pounded on the front door.

It wasn't Fred because even he couldn't be two places at one time.

As far as I knew.

George?

Grace blanched.

Fred, Grace, and I charged downstairs to the living room.

Fred got there first and opened the door.

"What are you doing here?" a screechy voice demanded.

"I might ask the same of you." Fred held the door and blocked the opening, but, by craning around just right, I could see under his arm.

It was the wife with the scrunched up face and bowl haircut. Ellen? Lynn? Alinn.

Grace came up behind me. I tried to block her view. She didn't need to meet this woman.

My efforts were futile. She was small and fast.

"Who are you?" Grace asked.

"Chuck's real wife, and I'm here to rescue my husband's parents from the woman who murdered him."

"What the hell's going on here?" Leon demanded.

"Is that my father-in-law? Are you Leon Mayfield?" Alinn tried to shove past Fred.

I waited for him to toss her out the door, but he stepped back instead.

Alinn rushed inside.

Grace pushed her outside.

She came back.

I'd seen Grace in action in one cat fight when her opponent was twice her size. I'd put my money on Grace.

Fred intervened, holding them apart. "Stop!"

They stopped.

"Alinn, what are you doing here?" he asked.

She looked past him, her gaze focusing on Leon. "I'm your son's wife, his first wife, his real wife, and I'm pregnant with his child."

Chapter Fifteen

Grace gasped. Her hand flew to her mouth.

Leon's jaw dropped so far his beard rested on his chest. He looked at Alinn then at Grace. "What the hell is she talking about?"

Grace turned to me, her eyes begging for help.

From me?

I turned to Fred.

"Alinn," he said, "your presence here is inappropriate. You need to leave."

"I'm not leaving without my husband's parents. Are you Leon and Edwina Mayfield?"

Leon nodded uncertainly. "Yeah."

She flung herself at him and wrapped her arms around him. "I'm so happy to finally meet you!" She released him and embraced Edwina. "Chuck told me so much about you two!"

And Chuck never lied.

Edwina tentatively returned the embrace. "He didn't tell us nothing about you."

Alinn took Edwina's hand. "We was going to. He said whatever problems you all had in the past, he knew you'd be excited about the baby. But we never got to." She pointed at Grace. "We never got to because that woman killed him."

Grace lunged toward her. Fred stopped her in mid-lunge.

"I didn't kill him!" Grace shouted. "I loved him and he loved me!"

Time for the best friend to step in. I planted myself in front of Alinn. "What are you doing here? How did you know Chuck's parents would be here? Have you been stalking Grace?"

Alinn drew herself up defiantly. She was still several inches shorter than I am. I scowled menacingly down at her.

"I went to the farm where my poor, dead husband grew up," she said. "I wanted to meet my in-laws so we could grieve together. The neighbors told me they'd gone to Pleasant Grove to see the woman who said she was married to their son. I got here as fast as I could to rescue my family before she could murder them too."

"You lying witch!" Grace's face flushed as she struggled to get free of Fred's hold.

I sent Fred a telepathic message to turn her loose. If she had any trouble taking down Alinn…which I doubted…I'd help. I'd love to see Alinn convulsing from the effects of my stun gun.

He didn't get the message or he ignored me.

Of course he got the message. He ignored me.

Alinn pulled a piece of paper from the back pocket of her faded slacks and handed it to Leon. "Here's a copy of our marriage certificate dated seven years ago."

Leon accepted the paper, unfolded it, and squinted at it for a long time. "You all get a divorce?"

Alinn put her hands on her hips and thrust out her belly. "No."

Leon looked at Grace. "You got one of them marriage papers?"

Grace strained against Fred's grasp. "Yes, I do."

"Can I see it?"

Again Grace looked at me.

Again I looked at Fred.

"You have no reason to see Grace's marriage documentation," he said. "She and Chuck were married last August by a Justice of the Peace in Crappie Creek, Missouri. There are some complicated legal issues in this situation which will have to be decided in a court of law, but that's not your concern."

Bless Fred's heart for trying to get Leon off Grace's case. Even I knew how the complicated legal issues would turn out. If Alinn was the first wife, absent a divorce, she was the legal wife. Grace's marriage license was of no consequence. And, as Fred so politely pointed out, none of Leon's business.

Leon stroked his beard. "What the boy said about a bunch of other women, it was true?"

Rickie had been downgraded...or maybe upgraded...from grandson to the boy.

"Seven women," Fred said.

Leon's narrow gaze darted back and forth between Grace and Fred. "Why'd he do that?"

To have more access to decongestants? To establish contact with more prison ministries? Because he liked variety? For once, I kept my mouth shut.

Alinn dropped her head. "I think it was because he wanted so bad to give you a grandbaby. We tried really hard, but it took me seven years to get pregnant. As soon as I told him about our baby, he said he was going to get rid of all those other women."

Grace's face fell and she slumped in Fred's arms.

I was married to the King of BS. I know BS when I hear it, and Alinn was rolling it out.

She also appeared to be under the influence of it. She still believed at least one of Chuck's lies, that her son would inherit from the wealthy parents who were desperate for a grandchild. She didn't seem to know they already had enough grandkids for a football team. Or maybe it was baseball. Whatever. They were not likely to be impressed with another grandbaby, and instead of being wealthy, they had been dependent on Chuck for money.

I had to get Alinn to take the Mayfields and run before she discovered the truth and left them to sponge off Grace.

How could I tactfully do that?

Alinn, please take these vermin and leave.

Tact is not my strong point.

"You've had a long day, Alinn, driving all over Oklahoma and—" Which state did she live in? We were in Missouri, so I couldn't go wrong with that one. "Driving through Oklahoma and Missouri and all those places. In your condition, you probably need to get home early. It's already nine o'clock. I can suggest some good motels close by."

She spun on me, squinchy eyes blazing. "It's only an hour to Leavenworth where I have a nice home." She looked disparagingly around Grace's living room. "I have pretty carpet, not this ugly, dirty old stuff. Chuck painted our walls so they're not dingy and nasty like yours, and I have a beautiful guest room already set up for my husband's family." She turned to the family in question. "Are you ready to get away from the woman who murdered your son?"

Anger replaced sadness on Grace's face and again she struggled to free herself. Fred held her with no show of effort. "I did not!" she shouted. "Maybe you killed him because he was leaving you to be with me!"

Alinn took a step toward Grace, and I groped in my purse for my purple stun gun.

"Which one of you's telling the truth?" Leon demanded.

Alinn went back to wrap an arm around his waist. "Ask her," she said. "Ask her if she's his legal wife. Ask her if he told her he was leaving her and all those other women because I'm pregnant."

Was she really pregnant? A small belly protruded from her scrawny frame, but it wasn't enough to say if she was pregnant or just didn't do sit-ups.

I didn't know, didn't care. Only wanted her and the Mayfields gone.

"Alinn's his legal wife," I said.

Grace's eyes widened in pain and shock at my betrayal.

"Grace is the love of his life," I hastily added. "They didn't need the laws of the land to bind their hearts because they were joined in love."

Alinn started toward me, fists and lips clenched. I was bigger than her, but she looked a lot meaner.

I held my stun gun toward her and zapped the air in a warning surge of power.

She stopped in her tracks.

"What the hell is that thing?" Leon asked.

"You don't want to get close enough to find out." I sent another electrical charge zinging through the air.

"The three of you are trespassing in Grace's house. Leave now or I'll use this on you!"

Alinn took Edwina's arm. "Let's get out of this trashy place."

The trio started toward the door, but Leon stopped and shot Grace a scathing look. "You lied to us!"

"I did not!"

I zapped the stun gun again. "Get out of here! Go! Now!"

They went.

Grace burst into tears.

Fred guided her to a chair.

I knelt beside the chair and placed a hand on her arm.

"Go away!" She slapped my hand. "You took up for that woman! Now Chuck's family hates me, and they're gone forever."

Fred shrugged helplessly. Fred can take down an armed villain with a swift kick. He can outwit murderers and con them into confessing. But when it comes to a crying woman, he's helpless.

"Grace, the truth was bound to come out," I said.

She cried harder.

"Trust me, you're better off without those people. They thought you would take up where Chuck left off, sending them money. They were going to take advantage of you."

She wailed.

Logic wasn't helping.

"Grace, I'm sorry if I hurt you."

"I'm glad they're gone." I hadn't seen Rickie come in.

Grace pulled her son into an embrace. "They were the only grandparents you'll ever have."

He wiggled free. "They're not my grandparents. I don't want any grandparents. They smelled bad like they hadn't taken a bath in a month. I bet they had lice."

Kid was smarter than I thought.

Grace forced a smile. "No, you don't need grandparents. We have each other."

"Whatever." He left the room.

Such a touching moment between mother and son.

Grace's smile turned to a frown when she looked at me. "See what you did to my son?"

What had I done to her son? Made him happy?

"Lindsay," Fred said, "you need to get some sleep. You're going to be exhausted at work tomorrow."

I stood. "Yeah. Right. I better go." Before Grace kicked me out.

Fred and I left.

Grace slammed the door behind us. I couldn't hear the new deadbolts turning, but I was sure she'd locked them all.

"She'll get over it," Fred assured me as we walked toward the street.

"I know."

"Do you?" he asked.

"No. I don't know. I don't care."

He didn't challenge my lie. "That was an excellent display of using your stun gun for maximum effect without harming anyone."

His white hair glowed in the moonlight almost like a halo. "Was that a compliment?"

"Of course."

159

Wow. The evening wasn't a complete loss. Fred had complimented my skills with a gun.

"Do you think Alinn is really pregnant?" I asked.

"I have no idea. But if she is, it doesn't belong to Chuck. There's a note in the autopsy report about his vasectomy."

Rickhead had one of those, but Rickie was proof it hadn't been successful. "Those have been known to fail."

"Not Chuck's. His vas deferens was severed."

Chuck had been sort of truthful with Grace. He really was sterile. He'd lied about the reason, but he'd completely lied to the other women. I needed to tell her that.

If she ever spoke to me again.

Chapter Sixteen

Fred walked me to my door because it was dark and he's a gentleman and evil people were about. I had my stun gun and was quite capable of defending myself, but I appreciated his gesture.

"Good night," I said.

"Open your door before I leave."

"Seriously? Do you think somebody's hiding inside?"

"It wouldn't be the first time."

I sighed melodramatically before unlocking and opening my front door.

He stepped inside briefly. "Nobody here. Good night."

After the drama of the evening, I wouldn't have minded a hug. Fred's not a hugger, and I wasn't about to admit to feeling needy. It was a ridiculous feeling anyway. Grace and I weren't real friends like Paula and I were. It didn't matter if she was angry with me. It was crazy that I felt guilty for playing a part in separating her from those awful people.

But I did. I felt guilty and sad and inexplicably lonely, as if I were experiencing Grace's loneliness.

I stood on the threshold of my empty house for a moment.

Of course it was empty since I wasn't inside yet.

A white streak came out of the darkness and rubbed against my leg. Henry knew I needed a bit of comfort. He's psychic, sometimes more so than Fred.

"Come in, big guy, and let's have a snack."

He trotted toward the kitchen.

One leg rub was better than nothing.

I turned on the light and followed him. After I poured food into his bowl, I checked my phone. Trent had called twice.

I wanted to talk to him. I needed to talk to him, hear a friendly voice, feel not alone. I needed him to tell me I'd done the right thing for Grace by getting rid of her in-laws.

I went to the living room and sank into my comfortable arm chair for a comfortable conversation.

"Missed you last night," I said as soon as he answered.

"Missed you too. How'd your day go? Sell a lot of chocolate?"

For his own good, I wasn't going to tell him about Fred's and my visit to Howdy Doody's place. He'd worry. Grace hadn't asked me to keep her in-laws a secret, so we could talk about them. "I got to meet Chuck's parents tonight." I told him about Leon and Edwina and how Alinn swooped in to claim them as hers. "Grace is pretty upset about all of it."

"Yeah, she has a lot going on in her life right now."

"You could say that. Her husband's been murdered, she may go to prison, and her husband's first wife just stole her in-laws. And now she blames me for them leaving."

"How about I come over for a while?"

162

"No." Yes! "It's late. We both need to get some sleep." I was being rational. Much as I wanted Trent to come over, I knew that would be silly.

"I understand. You have to get up really early. It's Wednesday. The weekend will be here soon. Get some sleep and try not to worry about Grace. Chuck's parents sound like terrible people. She's better off without them."

"She's lonely. She wants to have a family."

"She has Rickie."

"Who's going to take care of him if you cops put her in prison?" The confrontational question flew out of my mouth before I could stop it. That happens a lot.

Trent was silent for a moment. "His dad?"

"Yeah, right. We both know that's not going to happen. Are you still investigating Chuck's murder or have you decided you have the guilty person and you're not going to do anything else?"

He was silent for a longer moment.

"You're not doing anything, are you?" I demanded. "You've made up your mind Grace is guilty, and that's the end of it. You're going to ramrod her straight to the gas chamber."

"Get some sleep. Love you."

I pushed the "End Call" button as hard as I could. It wasn't nearly as satisfying as slamming down the receiver on an old phone, but it would have to do.

I was angry. With Trent? Maybe. With myself? Definitely.

Henry strolled into the room and meowed then headed for the stairs.

At least my cat and I were still on good terms.

᭡᭢᭞

The next morning while Paula and I worked I told her about Gaylord's wife and Chuck's parents and Alinn and how Grace wasn't speaking to me. I left out the part about me not speaking to Trent. I hadn't told him yet that I wasn't speaking to him, so it didn't count.

She slid a pan of cinnamon rolls into the oven. "Grace will get over it."

I set a stalk of bananas on the counter and began peeling them for my Chocolate Chip Banana Nut Brownies. Fruit, nuts, and chocolate in one delicious dessert. Practically health food. "I guess. But you should have seen how sad she was. She hasn't had a lot of luck in the family department."

"It doesn't sound like those people would have brightened her family experience. Grace will be fine. She's a survivor."

I hate it when somebody gives me logic instead of sympathy. I plopped another banana into my bowl. "She'll survive if she doesn't go to prison for killing Chuck."

"Well, yes, there is that. Have you heard anything else about the case against her?" Paula measured flour for biscuits into a large bowl.

"Trent and I had a very short conversation after I got home last night. He wouldn't tell me anything about the investigation or if there even is one. I think they've decided Grace is guilty, and they're not going to look any further. Thank goodness Fred and I are doing something." I assaulted the bananas viciously with a potato masher.

"Have you ever considered the possibility that Grace might be guilty?" Paula kept her attention focused on stirring the contents of her bowl, thus avoiding the visual scolding I sent her way.

"No."

My self-proclaimed best friend wasn't speaking to me. My real best friend didn't trust my judgment. My boyfriend and I were not on good terms. For all I knew, Fred and Henry could be mad at me now.

By 1:30 the lunch hour rush was winding down. Six people remained at the counter and four tables were occupied.

I handed a woman her change.

"The Chocolate Chip Banana Nut Brownie was wonderful," she said.

"Thank you. Glad you enjoyed it."

It always makes me happy to know my creations bring pleasure to people.

The satisfied customer left.

Paula moved up beside me and leaned close. "Look at that woman at the corner table." She inclined her head toward the end of the room farthest from the front wall of windows.

The woman at that table had short, curly gray hair, black-framed glasses, and wore a frumpy black dress that disproved the notion of black making a woman look slimmer. She was big, probably close to six feet and two hundred fifty pounds. She sat alone, staring at her plate, pushing around pieces of her Chocolate Chip Banana Nut Brownie.

"She looks lonely," I whispered. "We could give her a complimentary dessert to cheer her up, but the one she already has doesn't seem to be helping. My brownies deserve better treatment than that."

"She has a five-o'clock shadow."

"That's even sadder. Let's tell her she's our hundredth customer of the day and give her half a dozen cookies." That much chocolate should cheer up anybody.

"I think it's a man."

"Poor thing. No wonder she's alone. Struggling with gender identity has got to be tough."

"Something's not right."

"I can't believe you're being so judgmental." I took two chocolate chip cookies with nuts from the dessert display case and set them on a plate.

Paula laid a restraining hand on my arm, but I ignored her.

I approached the unfortunate person's table. "Good after…"

The person looked up. His sleeve slid down his arm exposing a tattoo of a heart with the lopsided initials "KD" inside it.

I almost dropped my plate of cookies.

Paula had called it. Something was wrong, bad wrong.

George held a finger to his lips.

He needn't have worried. I wasn't going to draw the attention of my normal customers to him.

"What are you doing here in that ridiculous outfit?" I whispered angrily.

"You gotta help me."

"No, I don't."

"If you don't help me, that crazy Gaylord Dumford's going to kill me."

"That is not my problem."

"Yeah, it is. Dumford wants the money I stole from him and buried in your basement. You gotta give it to me or he'll kill me."

I didn't have that money. His grandparents dug it up before they sold the house to me. They tucked it away safely in an account in the Cayman Islands, taking only some of the interest to repay all the money they'd spent trying to keep George out of prison. The rest was waiting for George to start college. Well, first he had to get his GED, but his grandparents were eternally optimistic.

If I told George's grandparents his life was in danger, they'd probably withdraw the entire amount and give it to him so he could give it to that disgusting Gaylord Dumford.

Dilemma. Let Dumford kill the Murrays' worthless grandson and upset Cathy and Harold or let Dumford have ten million dollars?

Even if he got the money, what guarantee would we have that he wouldn't kill George anyway? Howdy Doody didn't strike me as the kind of man whose word was his bond.

"I don't have that money. Do you think if I had ten million dollars, I'd be working this hard every day?" I would, actually, because I love making desserts and seeing the happiness my work brings to people.

His cold gaze constricted behind the phony glasses. "How did you know it was ten million?"

"Tiger Lily told me." A few other people, including his grandparents, had told me, but George didn't need to know that.

167

"You said she took it, but I talked to her. She said she didn't."

"I said she probably took it."

"Well, she didn't so it's still in your basement or you have it."

My mind was blank. No believable lies came to mind. "I can't talk. I've got customers." I spun around and headed back to the cash register with my cookies.

"I'll wait."

He did. Sat there playing with his food until the last customer left and Paula and I had taken all the dirty dishes except his to the kitchen.

I sighed and headed toward his table.

"Call the police," Paula said for the third time or maybe it was the fifth or sixth.

"I'll talk to him. Then we'll get rid of him one way or the other."

I filled two glasses with Coke, slid into a chair at George's table, and shoved one toward him. "Why are you wearing those weird clothes?"

"He's following me. Well, not him but one of his men. Maybe more than one of his men. I lost him at a thrift shop by coming out dressed like a woman."

I studied him closely. Sweat glistened on his forehead. The room temperature was sixty-eight degrees. I'd been rushing around so I had a sheen of sweat on my forehead too. However, George wasn't sweating from sitting in the corner, mangling my Chocolate Chip Banana Nut Brownie. He was genuinely frightened. Surely he wouldn't have gone out in public looking like that if he wasn't.

"George, I do not have your money. You're going to have to go to Plan B." I took a drink from my Coke.

"I already went to Plan B. You're the reason it didn't work."

I slammed my Coke on the table so hard some of it splashed out. "Seriously? I'm to blame because you can't find the money you stole and buried in the basement of the house I now own? I'm to blame because Plan B failed? Am I also to blame because you flunked second grade?"

"It was third grade, and how did you know about that?"

I slid my chair back and stood. "This conversation is over." Of course my curiosity got the better of me. "What was Plan B and why am I the reason it didn't work?"

"You stopped me from finding Chuck's money."

I sat again. "Dumford would have forgiven the ten million you stole from him if you brought him the money Chuck skimmed? How much did Chuck skim?" Grace hadn't mentioned how much money Chuck had left, but surely she'd have said something if it was ten million dollars.

George looked away.

"Don't lie to me," I warned. "If you lie to me, there's no chance I'll help you."

He leaned forward. "Chuck didn't skim any money."

"Wait. You said Dumford sent you to Grace's house to get back the money Chuck skimmed from him." If Chuck hadn't been stealing Howdy Doody's money, what reason did he have to kill him?

He shrugged. "Like you never told a lie?"

"My veracity isn't in question here. What were you doing in Chuck's house in the middle of the night?"

"I knew Chuck was saving up so he could quit the drug business. He didn't say how much he had, but I figured it was enough to get Dumford off my ass for a little while until I could find that money in your basement."

This time I slammed my fist on the table. Didn't want to waste any more Coke. "I'm only going to say this one more time, so you need to listen. There. Is. No. Money. In. My. Basement. Your girlfriend dug up the floor. Fred and I dug it up even more when we fixed it. You can dig all the way to the center of the earth, and you will find nothing but dirt, molten lava, and maybe a few skeletons of prehistoric men along the way!"

Silence.

Dishes rattled in the kitchen. I needed to finish with George and go help Paula.

I rose again. "Are we done?"

He dropped his head. His whole body sagged. "Yeah, we're done. I'm done. You ever heard the term walking dead man?"

I did not feel sorry for him.

I did not. He was a horrible man who brought this on himself.

I did feel sorry for the Murrays who would grieve for all the lost dreams they had for their grandson if Howdy Doody killed him.

But that was not my problem.

I started away from the table.

"Hey, you know that cop you're dating, the one you called last night?" George asked.

I turned back slowly. "What about him?"

"I might need to talk to him."

Was he going to blackmail me into helping him by threatening to rat me out over the stun gun episode in Grace's house? "What do you want to talk to him about?"

He pushed his wig back and ran a hand over his forehead. "If Dumford goes to prison, he can't kill me."

From what I'd seen on Investigation Discovery, I doubted that was true. Howdy Doody seemed the type criminal who could reach out from behind bars to put a hit on somebody. But I was interested to hear what George had to say. Howdy Doody was still my favorite suspect in Chuck's murder. Just because I didn't know what his motive was didn't mean he didn't have one. "Go on."

"If I deliver him to the cops, maybe they can put me in one of those witness protection things where I change my name and nobody can find me."

I returned to my seat, put my elbows on the table, and tented my fingers. "I'm listening."

"Get me an appointment with your boyfriend. I'll tell him everything I know about Dumford and his drug business."

"Trent's a busy man. I'm not going to bother him unless you convince me you've got something worth his time."

George sat upright. "Dumford's in charge of getting drugs into prisons in five states. I think that's going to be worth your boyfriend's time."

I shrugged and tried to appear casual. Inside I was chortling smugly that I would so easily be able to stomp on his self-importance. "You've got to do better than that. We already know about the church-to-prison connections and how Chuck's wives gave him access to all those different churches."

He scowled. The expression looked silly when combined with the wig and glasses. "If you know all that, why hasn't Dumford been arrested already?"

Because Fred had just come up with the theory the day before. "We like him for Chuck's murder." We being my ego and me. It was not my fault if George interpreted *we* to mean the cops and me. "We'd like to get evidence of both crimes before we move on him."

George didn't react.

"You could probably get a much better deal if you helped us find proof he's a murderer," I said.

"I don't know nothing about a murder."

I did that thing Fred and Trent do when questioning a suspect…waited quietly until he blurted out something.

It didn't work for me. George waited quietly too.

"Think that would be something you could help us with?" I finally asked.

"I don't know. Maybe. You think Dumford killed Chuck? Why would he do that?"

This conversation wasn't working out the way I'd hoped. "I…we thought at first he killed him because Chuck skimmed money from him, but you said you lied about that. Is it possible Chuck did steal money from Dumford, that your lie was true?"

"I don't know. Maybe."

I resisted the urge to yank off that stupid wig and zap his head with a million volts of electricity until his brain came to life. "Not good enough. We need something to go on. Did Chuck and Dumford fight?"

"How do I know? I've been in the joint for the last six years."

"You said Dumford wanted to come to your party so he could talk to Chuck. Why didn't he just call him? Show up at his door? Invite him over for dinner?"

George scratched his temple and tried to straighten the wig. He only made it worse. "I don't know."

I waited.

That time it worked.

"Chuck wanted out of the business. Dumford wanted him to stay in. He couldn't find anybody to replace him. Chuck had a lot of connections. He was Dumford's biggest distributor. Dumford's stuck with a lot of product he needs to get out there."

"Oh?" A brilliant, fully-formed idea burst onto the frontal lobe of my brain. Fred would be so impressed. "What if I could persuade Grace to take over Chuck's territory?"

"Grace? You think she'd agree to deal? She don't seem like the type."

Of course I didn't think she'd agree to deal drugs. But maybe she'd pretend to be interested if it meant we could get Howdy Doody to confess to Chuck's murder. "I'll talk to her. We're buddies." At one time.

George considered it for a moment then shook his head. "She's only one wife. Dumford needs more connections than that."

"We've connected with the other wives." In a way. "Grace has close connections with some of them."

"She has? That's strange."

Connected. There's an ambiguous word with lots of different meanings. Grace and Stella had been in a physical fight. Grace and Alinn had been in a verbal fight. Those are connections.

"Strange things happen. Deal with it. I'll talk to Grace and get this set up with her, then you need to deliver Dumford to her house. After that, I'll turn you over to Trent."

He clenched his fists. "I want to talk to the cop now." Big, hairy hands protruding from the sleeves of a dress failed to convey any real threat.

"And I want to drive a Porsche 911 and never get a speeding ticket." I took my phone from my pocket. "What's your number?"

George's bushy eyebrows lowered, and the wig crept halfway down his forehead. "You promise you'll get me a deal with Trent?"

"Maybe Dumford will confess to murder, then he'll get the gas chamber and you'll never have to worry about him again."

He gave me his number. I punched it into my phone and hit call.

He jumped then took his vibrating phone from his pocket.

I ended the call.

"Now you have my number and I have yours. Call me after you talk to Dumford."

Everything was falling into place. All I had to do was convince Grace to pretend to want to deal drugs. Okay, first I had to convince her to speak to me again.

I also had to tell Fred about my plan. I was certain he'd be eager to help and amazed at my brilliance.

And I probably needed to let Trent in on the scheme eventually.

My plan had a few potential glitches.

Chapter Seventeen

I arrived home that afternoon with three bags of chocolate…one to bribe Grace, one to bribe Fred, and one for my personal consumption. Taking down a murderer is stressful. All parties require a lot of chocolate.

The Mayfields' old truck was still parked in front of Grace's house.

A chilly wind greeted me when I got out of the car. It came from the direction of that truck.

Not really, of course. March in Kansas City brings days of sunshine and days of cold winds. The direction of the wind was a coincidence.

A black wall of clouds in the west suggested we might get rain, perhaps a storm, maybe even a tornado.

Or perhaps I was projecting my tempestuous thoughts onto the weather.

I went inside, fed Henry, then headed over to Grace's with one bag of chocolate. No point in talking to Fred until I made sure Grace would go along with the plan.

She opened the door as soon as I knocked.

"Lindsay!" She threw her arms around me. "I'm so sorry I was mean to you!"

Step One, convincing her to talk to me, had concluded successfully.

I hugged her back then held up the bag. "I brought chocolate! There's a big piece of cake in here and a couple of cookies."

She burst into tears and hugged me again. "You're such a good friend! Rickie loves your cookies!"

I disentangled myself and looked around. Her house showed signs of progress...fewer boxes, more personal items such as candles and a bright bouquet of silk flowers. "Is Rickie still hiding in his room?"

"He's at school. I took him this morning. I don't know what's going to happen to me, but I thought I should try to make his life as normal as possible while I'm still..." She gulped. "While I'm still free."

"About that..." I cleared my throat. "Let's sit down."

We both looked at the sofa. "In the kitchen."

"Good idea."

We passed the exact spot where I zapped George. A pleasant memory.

I set the bag on the table and took a seat while Grace got Cokes for both of us. She remembered to put in the Coke before the ice. I made a difference in someone's life.

She sat across from me and heaved a big sigh. "You were right."

"About the ice? Something I learned from years of drinking Cokes."

"No, the Mayfields. Rickie didn't like them either. He said I ought to thank you for getting them out of here."

One more thing Rickie and I agreed on. Scary.

I took the containers of cake and cookies out of my bag and set them on the table. "I have a plan to make that charge of murder against you go away."

"Did you find me a lawyer? I can pay for a good one."

"Better than a lawyer." I slid the desserts across the table toward her. "I've got a plan to catch the real murderer." I took a plastic fork from the bag and handed it to her. "Try the cake."

She hesitated then had a bite. "That's the best chocolate cake I've ever eaten."

"Thank you. George is going to tell Dumford that you want to take Chuck's place in the drug distribution thing, then—"

She stopped with the second bite of cake halfway to her mouth. "What?"

"Keep eating."

She hesitated but couldn't resist my cake.

While her mouth was full of chocolate, I continued. "You're going to pretend to be interested so we can get him over here and question him."

She shook her head.

"Have another bite of cake."

She set her fork on the table. "I don't think I can do that."

"Yes, you can." I took a cookie from the other container and offered it to her. "Don't you want to see Chuck's murderer brought to justice?"

She accepted the cookie. "When?"

"I don't know. Soon. George is going to call me when he gets the meeting set up."

"You'll be with me?"

"Of course. And Fred will too." I added a silent probably. "I'm going to talk to him right now."

Grace hesitated only a moment. "Okay. I got to leave now to pick up Rickie from school, but I'll be back in a few minutes."

That would give me time to talk to Fred.

We walked outside together. Grace got her car from the garage in the side yard and drove away.

I had to pass the Mayfields' truck again to get across the street. Would they come back for it or would Grace have to call the city to haul it away?

How long would they stay with Alinn before she wised up and kicked them out? Or before they wised up and left her?

The truck was a blemish on our lovely street, but at least those people were no longer at Grace's.

I dashed home, grabbed Fred's bag of chocolate, and went to his door.

He answered my knock immediately. "Please come in. I have an Australian Shiraz that will compliment your chocolate cake."

I didn't ask how he knew I had chocolate cake in the bag.

I went inside and set my bag on his coffee table beside the dessert plates.

"George came to the restaurant today dressed as a woman because he's afraid Dumford is going to kill him. Grace is going to pretend to want to deal drugs to lure him over here, and I need you to be there."

Fred poured two glasses of wine and handed one to me. "Take a deep breath. Drink some wine. Relax." He opened the bag and divided the contents between the two plates. "This is my favorite chocolate cake."

179

We were off to a good start.

I took a deep breath and a sip of wine. It was delicious. A punch of full flavor that lingered on the tongue with spicy notes.

Not really. I read that on the Internet. I only knew it tasted good.

I told Fred about my adventure with George and my plan to lure Dumford to Grace's house and get him to confess to murder.

"I see," he said.

I took another drink of wine and waited for the congratulations, the applause, the appreciation of my brilliance.

"How will you get him to confess?" he asked.

"I thought I should leave something for you to do. I don't want you to feel left out."

"Thank you. I have also had an interesting day. I helped Laurie and her daughters find a shelter for abused women. She's left her husband."

"Good for her!" I held up my glass in a salute, then slowly lowered my glass. "Oh. That may have an effect on our plan."

"You may find it difficult to get him over here. He will likely be running around the city searching for his wife and daughters. I don't think he's the type to give up any of his possessions easily."

"Does he know yet?"

Fred consulted his watch. "Probably not. He doesn't usually come home until after six."

I shot to my feet and grabbed my phone from the pocket of my jeans. "Probably? Usually? It's not like you to be so indefinite!"

"I didn't know Dumford's schedule would be of interest to you."

I found the call to George's phone and hit redial.

He answered immediately.

"Where are you?" I asked.

"Who is this?"

"It's me, your new partner in crime. Lindsay. Where are you?"

"I'm on my way to meet Dumford and try to set up this cockamamie scheme of yours."

"Where are you meeting?" I tried not to sound panicked. "Is he going home first?"

"Nah. We're going to the church. That's where he does business. He's got a secret room in the basement where he keeps the product."

"This cockamamie scheme of mine has to take place tonight. Dumford's wife left him."

A stream of curse words followed. George's grammar wasn't all that great, but he had a large vocabulary of swear words. I made note of a couple I'd never heard before so I could use them the next time I slammed a drawer on my finger or stubbed my toe.

"Are you swearing because Dumford's wife left him or because we need to execute the plan immediately?" I asked.

He blew out a long sigh. "Both. The last time Laurie tried to leave him, he went on a tear. Couldn't get anything done till he found her." He hesitated a second. "He beat her so bad she had to go in the hospital. He's got a temper. We need to get him out of the way fast. Tonight. Before he hears about Laurie."

"Get him to Grace's house. We'll do the rest."

"I'll let you know what time. Be sure your boyfriend's there."

He hung up.

I slid my phone back into my pocket and looked at Fred. "He beats her."

"She mentioned the physical abuse as well as the verbal, but she didn't elaborate. She's conflicted. She's very religious, and Dumford tells her it's God's will that she stay with her husband no matter what."

I twisted one side of my lip in a sneer. "God didn't tell me that."

"Nor did He tell me. Last time we chatted, He was quite clear that He did not approve of such behavior."

"Usually when somebody tells me he had a dialogue with God, I tell him we have drugs for that, but I kind of believe you."

Fred neither confirmed nor denied my assertion. "Your plan to get Dumford in prison may be Laurie's only chance to escape and lead a normal life."

He was in. That meant my plan had a chance of success.

Now all I had to do was get Trent's cooperation. All I had to do was break my promise to Grace and confess to everything I hadn't been telling him over the last few days then convince him he should come over and eavesdrop on the meeting between Grace and George.

There's always a catch to the best of cockamamie schemes.

"I guess I need to call Trent," I said.

"Yes, you do. Grace should be back with Rickie by the time you finish. We'll have enough time to get him to Paula's house."

"Paula's house? You want to dump Rickie on her? I have to work with her!"

"Do you have a better idea of what to do with him? Sophie's working late tonight."

He knew Sophie's work schedule. I didn't, and I'm the neighborhood busybody. Evidence of their relationship?

"I guess your basement's not an option?" I asked.

"You can call Paula when you finish speaking with Trent."

"Or I could call her now." Says a lot about my dread of talking to Trent that I'd rather call Paula and ask her to babysit Rickie.

She answered on the second ring.

"How would you like me to be indebted to you for the next twenty years?" I asked.

"I thought you already were."

"I probably am." I couldn't bribe her with chocolate. She was my official taster. She had all the chocolate she wanted. "I need a favor. I need you to babysit Rickie for an hour or two tonight."

She was silent for an hour...or maybe it was a couple of seconds. "All right."

"You will? Thank you!"

"One condition."

"You want him delivered in handcuffs?"

"Any bad habits he teaches Zach, you have to correct."

"Deal." How hard could it be to make a four-year-old forget swear words or get him on Nicorette to kick cigarettes?

I gave Fred a thumbs-up.

Now all I had to do was talk to Trent.

I stared at my phone.

"You have to touch the screen to make it work," Fred said.

I felt a little thrill. Fred had learned something else from me. Sarcasm.

"I have to work up to this," I said.

My phone vibrated. For an instant I thought it was making calls on its own.

A text message had arrived.

On way.

George.

I showed the message to Fred. "They're on their way!"

"You've run out of time to work up to your call with Trent."

My phone burst into the theme song from Game of Thrones, my generic ring tone. "Hello?"

"It's Grace. Rickie and I are home now. You hear any more about me pretending to be a drug dealer?"

"Yes, the plan is a go. They're on their way. Fred and I will be at your house in a few minutes."

"On their way? Tonight? Are you sure this will be okay? I'm a little nervous."

"It's going to be fine. You can do it." I decided to deliver the news of Rickie's impending relocation in person. No need to increase her worry.

I straightened my spine and called Trent.

"Hi." He had a smile in his voice.

I didn't want to take away that audible smile by telling him everything I hadn't been telling him the last few days. Besides, with George and Dumford on their way, I didn't have time for all that.

"Hi. Got an anonymous tip for you. If you set up recording equipment outside Grace Mayfield's house immediately, you'll find out who killed Chuck. Love you! Bye! Oh, and you'll get information about a church basement full of drugs. Bye!"

I hung up.

Fred rolled his eyes.

My phone rang.

Trent.

"Answer it."

I wasn't sure if the command came from Fred or my own mind or both.

I answered.

"Lindsay, whatever you're up to, you can't do it."

"You didn't believe the anonymous call bit, huh?"

"Anonymous tipsters don't call from your phone and say they love me."

"It was worth a shot."

"What's going on?"

"I don't have time to tell you. George Murray and Gaylord Dumford are on their way to Grace's house right now."

Trent said some swear words. He didn't know as many as George, but he was no slacker. "Those men are dangerous. Take Grace and Rickie to your house, lock the doors, and stay inside. Please."

"I can't do that. I don't have time to explain. You need to trust me."

"You need to trust me. You're getting involved in something very dangerous."

I sensed he was close to breaking his vow of silence about all things police related. "You're going

185

to have to be a little more specific before I take you seriously."

"Gaylord Dumford is under investigation. That's all I can tell you."

"I can tell you more. He's coming to Grace's house tonight, and George is going to make him take us to a basement full of drugs." George didn't exactly say that, but I figured Fred could make him do it. "I'm going to Grace's house now. If you want to protect me from the big, bad drug dealers, you need to be there."

I hung up.

Chapter Eighteen

Fred and I walked out his front door into a rapidly darkening evening. The scuttling gray clouds warned of an unquiet night ahead. As we passed the Mayfield's ugly truck, an icy west wind slapped me across the face.

A shiver ran down my spine.

"If they don't come back for it soon, I'll call the city and have it towed," Fred said.

"What?"

"The truck. You shuddered when we walked past it."

"Oh. Yeah. I guess I did." We started down Grace's sidewalk. "Do you have a plan for tonight?"

"You're the one with the plan. George will coerce Dumford into taking us to the church basement full of drugs while you force him to confess to Chuck's murder."

"Well, yeah, that's the general idea, but I thought you might have a few of the details worked out."

"I'll follow your lead."

Thunder crashed.

I don't believe in omens.

Not usually.

We reached Grace's front door and Fred knocked.

Grace appeared, eyes wide, hair in disarray. "I'm so glad you're here! This is kind of scary."

I decided not to mention Dumford's physical abuse of his wife. No point in adding to Grace's fears. "It's going to be fine, but we should probably take Rickie over to Paula's."

Her eyes got wider. "Why?"

"Bad language," I said. "He may hear some bad language from these bad men." After George's outburst on the phone, I thought he might know some words even Rickie didn't.

"Rickie!" she called over her shoulder. "He's in his room, studying."

I wasn't about to ask what he was studying. The art of making bombs? How to take over the world in six easy lessons? He could be writing that one.

Rickie strolled down the hall, phone in one hand and a Coke in the other. "Yeah?"

"Remember Paula, the lady who works with Lindsay?" Grace asked.

"The one with the kid?"

"You're going to visit them for a little while."

"Why? What are you going to do that you want to get rid of me?"

"We don't want to get rid of you." Grace looked at me for help.

I hate it when that happens.

"We're going to have visitors and conduct some business," Fred said.

"Cool," Rickie said. "I need to learn about business."

"Everyone in the room must be of legal age to enter into a contract or the business transactions will be invalid."

Fred's legal training was showing…a few big words and a lot of BS.

Rickie studied him intently then shrugged. "Whatever. I like the kid. We'll have fun."

That sounded ominous.

"Lindsay will take you," Fred said.

"I know the way." He headed for the door.

I went after him. "You need me to get past the security system. Your fingerprints are on the blocked list."

He looked over his shoulder at me. "I don't believe you."

But he wasn't sure.

"Come on." I went with him.

"I wish those damned people would come get that freaking truck." He used a different word for freaking.

"Watch your language."

"Okay."

Damn! "Where did you pick that up?"

"What?"

"Saying okay when you mean you're going to do whatever you please and just want the speaker to shut up about it?"

"I heard you do it a few times. Pretty cool."

I wasn't sure what to think about that. On the one hand, it was pretty cool that he copied me. On the other hand…well, it was Rickie.

We arrived at Paula's front door. I knocked then pressed my index finger against the peephole.

"Lindsay?" Paula called from inside.

I took away my finger and looked at Rickie. "See? Told you."

Paula opened the door. "Rickie. How nice to see you. Please come in."

"Where's the kid?" He pushed inside.

Paula leaned close to my ear. "You owe me big time," she whispered.

"I know."

I went back to Grace's house.

A man stepped out of the shadows on the side of the house.

An image of Dumford beating Laurie to a pulp flashed across my brain. I yanked my phone and my stun gun from my pockets.

"What is that?" asked a familiar voice. Trent.

"Cell phone." I stuffed the stun gun into my back pocket.

He came closer. "The other one?"

"Good timing. George and Dumford will be here any minute. George wants to make a deal with you for immunity if he turns in Dumford for dealing drugs."

"Immunity? What has George done other than try to dig up your basement?"

"Well, actually, it's to save his life. Dumford wants to kill him. It's a long story."

Trent crossed his arms over his chest. "Go on."

"I can't! They'll be here any minute. Since you're here before they are, you can hide inside instead of out here. It's going to rain."

A flash of lightning and a rumble of thunder punctuated my prediction.

"Lindsay—"

"Hurry! They're going to be here any second!" I turned my back on him, ran to the door, and knocked.

Grace peeked out. "Oh, it's you. I thought it was them."

"Trent's here too." I looked over my shoulder, relieved to see he had followed me.

She held the door open. "Where's your partner?" she asked Trent. "Didn't you bring backup?"

He gave me one of those looks. "I wasn't given enough information to justify bringing somebody else into this situation."

"I'm glad you're here," Grace continued. "Lindsay's such a good friend to set this up so we can prove I didn't kill my husband. Dumford did it because Chuck was getting out of the drug business so he could take care of Rickie and me." She sounded almost as if she believed her declaration. Almost.

"Lindsay got you involved in this too, Fred?" Trent asked.

Fred stood beside the sofa. "You know how she is when she makes up her mind to do something."

He could have said he believed in this mission instead of focusing on my obstinate nature. I saved my reprimand for later.

"Trent, where do you want to set up?" I asked. "Coat closet? Kitchen? One of the bedrooms upstairs?"

"I'm not hiding in the coat closet."

"You're right." Always a good idea to agree with everything a person says when trying to get that person to cooperate. "With this weather, they may be wearing coats and we'll have to open that door. How about the kitchen?"

He made no move toward the kitchen. "Lindsay, we need to talk."

"Later."

"Now."

"Fine." I took his arm and led him into the kitchen.

He closed the door behind us.

Not a good sign.

"Sorry, we don't have time to make out," I said.

He didn't laugh. "Our guys are working with the Jackson County Drug Task Force to get an undercover agent in Gaylord Dumford's organization. So far we haven't been able to." He drew in a deep breath and slowly released it then took my hands in his. "You're getting into something very dangerous."

"You're here, Fred's here." And I have a stun gun in my back pocket. "It's going to be fine. We'll get Gaylord to take you to the church basement full of drugs, then you won't have to worry about the undercover agent."

Trent grimaced. "We were pretty sure that's where they stored the drugs, but we haven't been able to get enough evidence for a search warrant."

"Well, then…oh. Dumford's not going to invite you in. He met you at my place and knows you're a cop."

"Exactly. Best case scenario, you see what we already know is there, but your word isn't enough. Worst case…"

I was glad he didn't finish his sentence. I didn't want to hear any worst case scenarios.

Grace pushed through the door. "They're here! What do I do? What do I say?"

Too late to back out. "Tonight we're taking down Gaylord Dumford," I promised Trent. "I'll get the door," I promised Grace. Suddenly I was making promises all over the place.

I tried to pull my hands free of Trent's. He held on.

A cold wind swept through the room. The front door was open.

"Good afternoon, gentlemen," Fred said.

"Get out of here!" I whispered. "Dumford will recognize you!"

Trent released my hands and stepped out of view of the open doorway. We weren't touching anymore, but I could feel powerful waves coming from him. Waves of love? Anger? Both?

"Who are you?" demanded Howdy Doody from the other room. "Where's Chuck's woman?"

"I'm here!" Grace called. "Come on!" she whispered.

We raced into the living room.

George and Howdy stood inside the door, dripping on the ugly carpet.

Lightning flashed. The lights flickered causing their faces to move with the shadows as though demons battled beneath their skin. Thunder boomed somewhere close.

I shivered and decided I believed in omens after all.

Dumford's contorted face took malevolence to new heights. "I know who you are. You live across the street." He pointed at Fred. "That guy was at your party. What are you doing here?"

"I'm Grace's sister. Can't you tell by the hair?" Good grief. I'd just promoted myself from best friend to sister.

"I don't care if you're her guardian angel. I thought this was going to be a business meeting, not a freaking party."

He didn't say freaking. Good thing Rickie wasn't there. Those two might bond over their favorite swear word.

"I am Grace Mayfield's partner," Fred said. "Surely you didn't think this was her first venture into this particular business arena."

Grace gasped.

Howdy Doody frowned.

Fred remained neutral.

"It's all good, man," George said. "We can trust Lindsay and Fred." He sounded nervous. Fear of Dumford or fear of my stun gun?

Howdy finally shrugged. "Let's get on with it. I got things to do."

As he hulked past me into the room, I found it hard not to cower. I hadn't paid that much attention to him before. His resemblance to the old children's puppet had made him comedic. Now his large size, slightly stooped shoulders, and broad, angry face were intimidating.

"Please be seated." Fred indicated the sofa.

Nobody moved for a long moment.

Finally George went to the far end of the sofa and sat.

Dumford sat on the other end.

Chuck died on that sofa. Leon and Edwina sat on it. Howdy Doody and George were on it now. It would have to be exorcised before we burned it.

Grace settled tentatively in the arm chair across from George. That left one chair. I looked at Fred. He inclined his head toward the chair. I sat. He stood. I should have known. Vantage point. Looking down on everybody.

"Can I get you all something to drink?" Grace offered.

Bless her heart. Sitting in a room with drug dealers and a possible murderer, and she remembered her manners.

"I think not," Fred answered. "I'm sure these gentlemen are eager to get this business transaction brokered so they can move on to other things."

I would have killed for a Coke, but I thought it best not to bring up the k word among these people.

Fred folded his arms. "Mrs. Mayfield is willing to enter into a partnership with you, Mr. Dumford, in which she will perform in the same capacity as did her deceased husband, Chuck Mayfield. For her services in such capacity, she will receive the same remuneration as you paid to her deceased husband."

Dumford's lower lip hung slightly open increasing his resemblance to a puppet. "Huh?"

George cleared his throat. "Like we talked about, she's going to visit the churches and take our...um...stuff to them like Chuck did."

Dumford shifted his gaze to Grace.

She looked down and toyed with the hem of her shirt. Not the picture of confidence.

"You want the same money Chuck got?" Dumford asked. "You're just a woman."

I reached for my stun gun, ready to show him what it meant to be just a woman.

Fred stepped between Dumford and me.

Grace sat erect and smoothed her shirt. She hadn't liked Howdy's insult any better than I had. "Chuck told me all about his business. I know who his contacts are and how to get in touch with them, and I know what you paid him. I want the same pay."

She sounded so positive, I wondered if Chuck really had told her all that. Had she known more about him than she admitted?

Dumford cracked his knuckles. "Chuck got a bigger percentage than my other men because he did a better job. You got to prove yourself before I pay you what I paid him."

Grace quirked her upper lip in a sneer. "Three distributions at half the percentage to prove myself, then you increase my pay to Chuck's rate."

"Three distributions and I bump it up ten percent. After six, you get what Chuck was getting."

"Deal," she said.

Grace had risen to the occasion.

Was Trent able to hear all this? He could have left by the back door, but I figured he'd stick around to keep me out of trouble. Even if he was hearing all this, it probably wouldn't be enough to arrest Howdy Doody. It was a start, but we had to push for more.

Fred tilted his head in Dumford's direction. "Mrs. Mayfield will, of course, be allowed to inspect the product before she distributes any of it."

Howdy Doody laughed.

George made a sound somewhere between a giggle and a sob.

Grace folded her arms in imitation of Fred. "I'm not giving anybody anything unless I know it's clean and safe. I want to see where it comes from."

196

Howdy Doody stopped laughing.

I folded my arms also. We were a united, fierce force. "You got something to hide?"

Howdy glowered menacingly.

"Chuck told me bad meth can kill whoever takes it," Grace said. "He was careful. That's what made him a success. I'm going to be just as careful."

Again I wondered if she was making up this stuff or if Chuck really had confided in her.

It didn't matter as long as Dumford believed her.

He continued to glower but finally nodded. "When do you want to go?"

"Now. My son's daddy is dead and I need to make a living to support him."

Dumford harrumphed. "Chuck wasn't that kid's daddy."

I could almost see the steam coming from Grace's head. Howdy Doody was digging himself in really deep. Grace's hair color might come from a box, but she had the red-head spirit.

I caught her eye and gave a mini-shake of my head. We'd have time to smite him later. For now we had to play nice until we got what we needed.

Grace stood. "Let's go. We don't have all night."

George stood.

Dumford remained seated.

Grace sat back down. "You're not the only game in town."

She was doing a great job bluffing.

I was pretty sure she was bluffing.

"Yeah," I said, "that guy who came by yesterday to recruit you…what was his name?"

"Malcom Frost," she said without hesitation.

197

"Yeah, him. He was dressed for success." I scanned Howdy Doody's rumpled khakis and plaid shirt. "He was a good looking guy."

"Lindsay," Fred said, "this isn't about looks. This is about whose product is superior."

Dumford shot to his feet. "My stuff's the best. Who the hell is this Frost guy? I never heard of him."

"Grace," Fred said, "you did tell Mr. Dumford you would look at his product and give him a chance. I think you owe him some loyalty since your deceased husband worked for him."

Interesting how he did that, turned things around so Grace was doing Dumford a favor.

"Is it still raining?" Grace asked. "I don't want to get my hair wet."

"Take an umbrella," Dumford said.

We all started toward the door.

Dumford stopped. "This ain't no freaking party." He pointed to Grace. "Me and George and her. The rest of you stay here."

Fred moved between Grace and him. "There seems to be a misunderstanding. Mrs. Mayfield does not make business decisions without my presence."

"And my sister doesn't go anywhere without me," I said.

Dumford looked at all of us but said nothing. I held my breath. Was this going to be a deal-breaker? We could follow them, but I didn't think she should be alone with him and George. She might lose her courage. Dumford might lose his temper. We might lose track of his car in the dark, rainy night.

"I got a Cadillac Escalade," he finally said. "You'll all fit."

198

"But you do not have a chauffeur's license," Fred said. "The women will ride with me."

Dumford blinked slowly but didn't challenge Fred. He and Fred were the same height. He had at least fifty pounds on Fred, but Fred was blatantly the Alpha.

Dumford was a bully. He beat his wife, someone half his size. If Fred hadn't been there, he would probably have tried to intimidate Grace and me. In that event, I would have had to zap him. All bullies are cowards when someone stands up to them.

We left the house, the whole freaking party of us, and headed out into the dark and stormy night.

Chapter Nineteen

Fred left Grace and me on the porch while he got his car. I wanted to call Trent and find out where he was, whether he was coming with us, if he was getting all this, if he was ever going to speak to me again. But Howdy Doody might see me on the phone.

He and George waited in his white tank until Fred drove up behind him.

Grace and I charged through the rain and slid into the back seat of Fred's Mercedes.

"We're wet," Grace said. "I hope we don't ruin your upholstery."

"It's leather." He eased into the street behind Dumford's vehicle. "And treated against stains."

"That's so he can haul bodies in here," I said.

Grace gulped. "Really?"

Fred didn't answer.

I called Trent.

He answered.

"Where are you?" I asked.

"Two car lengths behind you. I don't have a lot of hope we'll be able to get evidence against Dumford, but if he tries to kill you, I can claim exigent circumstances and rush in to save your life."

"So if my life is in danger, you can break down the door to save me? You don't have to have a warrant? Let's talk about exigent circumstances."

"We're not going to talk about them, and you're not going to create them."

"I'll be fine. I can take care of myself. Anyway, Fred's here."

"If he wasn't, I'd put you in handcuffs and drag you away."

"That sounds kinky. We can talk about that later."

"Would you be serious? This is dangerous."

"Gotta go! Fred's calling me!"

"No, he's not!"

"No, I'm not."

I ended the call. "Trent's right behind us."

"This might work," Grace said. She sounded surprised.

We followed Dumford and George across town, past the suburbs, to a compound. Maybe I wouldn't have thought of it like that if I didn't know what was going on there.

Several buildings surrounded a large church with an elaborate steeple. Rain sparkled and danced in the flood lights. A charming place if I didn't know...but I did know.

Dumford pulled up in front of the Messianic Resurrection Church.

Fred parked next to him.

The rain had slowed to a drizzle.

We followed Dumford and George up the wide steps. George looked back, one eyebrow raised in a question. I nodded reassuringly. I was ninety-nine percent certain Trent was somewhere close. Maybe ninety-eight. Approximately.

Dumford withdrew a key and unlocked the tall, elaborately carved wooden doors.

"Must have a very affluent congregation," I said.

"I don't think they built this from members' tithes," Grace whispered.

One of these days I'd have to teach her about sarcasm.

The auditorium was large. Soft light from the wall sconces revealed plush crimson seats, stained glass windows, and a sanctuary at the front. The place was beautiful and felt hushed and reverent, the way a church should…not the way a drug storage unit would.

We didn't linger but headed down to the basement, a large open space with a tiled floor and folded tables on one side. Doors opened to rooms on the other side. Did Laurie's daughters attend Sunday School in those rooms? What were they teaching them? How to cook meth? Proper etiquette for serving it to guests? Thank goodness my fictional daughter wouldn't be going there.

We went through the basement to a well-appointed kitchen and a pantry loaded with large cans of green beans, tomatoes, soups, and a lower shelf of cleaning supplies. It all looked like the kitchen of a normal church where meals would be prepared for fellowship, weddings…and funerals.

Was Dumford really taking us to his meth storage or was he luring us to a secret passage where we would be slaughtered and our bodies never recovered? If Trent saw me go in this place and not come out, would that constitute exigent circumstances? What would Henry do when I didn't return home to let him in the house and feed him? Find another home? Was that how he came to me in the first place?

"Lindsay?" Fred's voice pulled me back to the situation at hand.

Dumford, George, and Grace stood in a dimly lit room behind the pantry, looking back at Fred and me. Mostly at me since I was in front of Fred. George's forehead glowed. He needed to do something about that tendency to sweat when he was scared.

I entered the room with confidence knowing I had a cell phone in one pocket, a stun gun in the other, and Fred behind me.

I had expected a huge area with large bags stacked to the ceiling and a narrow path to walk between them. The reality was much less impressive. Smaller than my extra bedroom. Boxes sat on shelves at one end of the room, the same type shelves as in the pantry behind us. Large bottles—some empty, some containing various amounts of ugly liquids—littered the floor along with bits and pieces of debris.

Dumford reached into one of the boxes and withdrew a plastic bag containing white crystals. "This is good stuff. I got a great cook. Nobody's ever complained."

He didn't say nobody had ever died from it. Dead people don't complain.

Fred took the package from him, opened it, and sniffed.

"Hey!" Dumford protested.

"My client told you we need to verify the product." He took out a half-inch crystal then returned the bag to Dumford. From his shirt pocket he produced a glass test tube.

Who carries a test tube in his pocket?

Fred.

He put the crystal in the tube then retrieved a bottle of bleach from the floor. "I hope your church won't mind," he said. "I borrowed this from the pantry. I only need a small amount. Grace, would you please take off the lid for me?"

As though this was routine, Grace unscrewed the top of the bleach bottle and stepped back.

Fred poured some into the test tube. The crystal jumped around frantically and dissolved. "Looks good."

Grace turned to Dumford. "I'm ready to make a deal."

Hard to believe this was the same woman who'd been nervous half an hour ago. Grace had hidden talents.

She and Fred worked out the details of their deal with Dumford while George sweated and I gave him reassuring looks. At least, that was my intent. I knew Trent was around even though I'd seen no sign of him. That was the whole idea, that he could spy on us and stay hidden.

But could he see us or hear us down in this basement?

Even if he was hearing all this, would it be enough for him to make an arrest?

We needed to walk out with drugs in hand...drugs in Dumford's hands.

"She'll take that box." I pointed to the middle of the shelves.

"What?" Dumford, Grace, and George all spoke at once.

Grace recovered first. "Yes. That's the one I want. Third row down, middle of that shelf." She looked at me as if for confirmation.

It didn't matter. Any box filled with illegal drugs would do, but it's always best to be specific. "That box is in the Feng Shui position. Grace is big into Feng Shui. It's been a guiding force in her life for many years."

"That's right. Fungus on that box. I want it."

"You want the whole box your first time?" Dumford asked.

This might be an opportunity to get Dumford's confession to Chuck's murder. I did the folded arms things again and glared at the Puppet Man/Drug Lord. "She's got a growing boy at home. You took his daddy away from her. The least you can do is give her the chance to make as much money as he made."

"Yeah," Grace agreed. "You killed my husband. You owe me this."

Dumford scowled. "I didn't kill Chuck. The cops arrested you for that. I'm giving you a chance to help us both, but I don't owe you nothing. This whole deal is off if you go to prison."

My first attempt to get a confession didn't work too well, but there would be time for that later. For the moment, I'd focus on the drug charges.

I walked over and peered into the box in question then tugged it toward me. "It's heavy. Too heavy for Grace. You carry it upstairs."

Dumford's scowl deepened. He thrust a thumb in Fred's direction. "You're her manager. You carry it for her."

"That's not in my job description," he said. "My union would take me to court if I did that."

"Your…union?"

"United Association of Managerial Workers of America, Local 247. If we didn't have a strict differentiation of duties, the efforts of everyone involved in the revolution would have been squandered. Don't you agree?"

One does not disagree with Fred, especially when he descends into jibber-jabber.

Dumford turned to George. "Carry the damned box."

George froze. He knew a cop was outside. He didn't want to be caught in possession of drugs. His eyes shifted from Dumford to me to Grace and back to me.

Why were people always looking to me for answers?

If George carried the drugs outside, that would not prove Dumford's guilt or contribute to George's innocence. "Really?" I said. "You're going to trust him to carry something that valuable?"

Fred put a hand on my shoulder. "I'm sure George will be able to take the merchandise upstairs without a problem."

George's eyes bulged to the point I expected them to fly out of his head.

I knew Fred had a plan. I winked at George, hoping to reassure him. He didn't look reassured.

He picked up the box.

Fred led us through the kitchen and up the stairs.

As we neared the church door, I became a little nervous about Fred's plan. He was cutting it close. The exit was only a few feet away.

Dumford moved ahead to unlock the door.

Fred fell back to walk beside George then leaned toward him as if to whisper in his ear.

George tripped. The box of drugs flew across the floor, spilling white packets everywhere. George landed face-first on the carpet.

Dumford stormed back to the mess. "What the hell?" He had more to say, a lot of words inappropriate for a church. "Get up!" Dumford started tossing packets back into the box. "Get up and help!"

George staggered to his feet. "I think my knee's broke!"

Fred looked innocent. Not that he ever looks guilty.

Dumford cursed some more as he refilled the box then picked it up. "If you want something done—"

"Do it yourself," I finished for him. "I told you not to trust him."

My remark earned me a snarl from Dumford. "Least you can do is open the door for me, idiot."

George limped forward to comply.

Dumford hauled his box of drugs through the door.

George started out, but Fred yanked him back, closed the door, and turned the key Dumford had left in the lock.

"Police! Put the box down and raise your hands!"

I recognized that voice. The good guys were here.

"Open the #$%^&* door!"

I recognized that voice too. The bad guy was locked outside with his bad drugs.

It was a good night.

Chapter Twenty

"Fred, open the door!" I said. "Trent may need our help!"

Fred didn't budge. "I doubt it."

"Clear!" Trent called.

Fred opened the door.

Cops streamed in, at least a hundred.

Maybe it was more like three.

"Show them to the basement, George," Fred directed.

As far as I knew, Fred and Trent had not talked. How had Fred known to close the door and lock Dumford and his drugs outside? This event was too well-choreographed to have happened without some planning. When did that planning happen? Why wasn't I a part of it?

Later I would demand answers, but at the moment, I needed to see what was going on. I pushed past Fred and out the door.

"You can't do this to me!" Two uniformed officers dragged Dumford down the church steps in handcuffs. "I didn't do anything! This is a setup! This is all that bitch's fault! If I go down, she goes down with me!"

I looked behind me at Grace. "You did a great job! He still believes you!"

One corner of her mouth tilted slightly upward. Close to a smile. "I guess I did, except he never confessed to killing Chuck."

"Not yet. He will."

"Take these damn handcuffs off me," Dumford bellowed. "I'm a deacon in this church! I been framed! This was all that bitch's idea! She didn't care about Mayfield! She wanted money! I can give you names, lots of names. I'll give you her name. I'll give you my cook's name."

For somebody who didn't do anything, had been set up and framed, he seemed to have a lot of information he was willing to spill.

"Are you okay?" Out of the darkness and gloom, Trent appeared at my side.

"Of course." I tried to sound as if the whole event had been inconsequential, as if I'd always been certain of the outcome and never once scared out of my wits. "You believed me. You brought the entire Pleasant Grove Police Department."

"Not quite everybody." He pulled me close. "I was worried about you."

"Have we got a deal?" George intruded on my post-crisis interlude with Trent. "You wouldn't have caught Dumford without me. I showed those other guys where the drugs are stored."

"I'm not sure what kind of deal you want to make," Trent said. "As far as we've been able to determine, you aren't guilty of any criminal acts. Your parole officer probably wouldn't like to hear about the people you've been associating with, but we can keep that between you and me if you stay out of trouble."

"Just be sure you don't make a deal with him!" George thrust an arm toward the squad car in the lot below where officers were shoving a protesting Dumford into the back seat. "He wants to give up other people so you'll let him go. If you let him go, he'll kill me!"

"I'll do the best I can. Even if the DA decides to cut him a deal in exchange for names, I don't see him getting off without some prison time."

George clenched his fists. "Some prison time? What does that mean? That he could come after me in a year or two?"

"I doubt it, but I can't promise anything. Maybe you could give us the names before Dumford does. Then he won't have anything to bargain with."

George dropped his hands to his sides. "It's been too long. I don't know anybody anymore."

George Murray was a totally despicable person. A drug dealer who'd played on the sympathies of his grandparents, stolen from another drug dealer, broken into Grace's house, tried to dig up my basement. I did not feel sorry for his plight.

"If you'd been paying more attention, you'd realize the idiot is trying to give up Grace," I said. "He still thinks she's really a drug dealer. That's not going to get him anywhere."

"He's got other names, real names."

"We'll get him to admit he killed Chuck. He won't be able to deal himself out of that one."

The mist of rain surrounding us became a mist of silence.

211

"We all know he did it." I broke the silence. "Who else? You've got him. All you have to do is make him confess."

"We'll figure it out," Trent said. "George, you want to ride with me to the station so we can get your statement?"

"What?" I snapped. "You're going to the station? Now?" We'd made it through the I've-got-a-secret phase. It was time to go back to a normal relationship. I wanted to take him home with me, hold him close, at least for the hours remaining before I had to go to work.

"Yes, now. I've got a lot of paperwork to do."

I sighed. I used to think cops spent all their time chasing bad guys who robbed banks or innocent women who happened to be going a few miles over the arbitrary and ridiculous speed limit. Only after I became involved with Trent did I realize how much time they spend filling out forms.

Grace moved down the steps to stand on Trent's other side. "You'll make him admit he killed Chuck, won't you?"

"I'll do what I can."

I'll do what I can? That was not the same thing as, Sure or Will do or No worries, I got this.

"Call me when you finish with him," I said. This conversation was far from over.

"It's getting close to your bedtime. I don't want to keep you up."

"I am so wired, I won't be able to sleep even with a bottle of wine!"

He grinned. "Okay. I'll call you."

"Are you finished with us, Detective Trent?"

I'd forgotten about Fred. He loomed behind George. He was taller anyway, and standing on a higher step made him appear large and ominous in the mist.

"You're taking Lindsay and Grace home?" Trent asked.

"Yes," Fred replied.

Trent gave me a quick kiss on the top of my damp, frizzy head. "I'll call you as soon as I can."

He and George went to his dark blue sedan. George was no longer limping. Apparently his knee wasn't broke after all.

"Ready?" Fred asked.

"Yes," Grace said immediately.

I watched Trent and George drive away.

The evening felt anti-climactic. Such a huge upheaval for what appeared to be minimal results. Dumford would be sent to prison for an undetermined amount of time. His wife would be safe for that time. George would be safe, though George would probably get into trouble again and might even have to share a prison cell with Dumford. That was on him. He'd helped us and we'd helped him. We were square.

Everything was wrapped up in a neat little package.

Except it wasn't.

"Lindsay?" Fred held a hand toward me.

"I'm coming."

❧❧

Fred walked me home then left with Grace to go to Paula's house and retrieve Rickie.

Henry waited on my front porch. He'd been out and about in the evening's rain, but he was completely

213

dry. He always does that, walks through the rain without getting a drop on him. Supernatural powers.

I gave Henry some catnip then wandered through the house. I should go upstairs to bed, but I had told the truth about being wide awake and wired. I went to the refrigerator and poured a glass of pink wine then watched out the window as Fred, Grace and Rickie crossed the street to Grace's house.

Fred headed back to his own place. He waved as he passed my house. Did he know I was watching? If I touched his hair, would it be dry like Henry's?

I took my glass of wine to my recliner. It tasted dull. Can wine go dull?

Henry stood at the foot of the stairs and looked at me. He was ready to go to bed. I needed to go to bed. He turned away from me and headed upstairs. I couldn't see his eyes, but I was pretty sure he was rolling them.

My phone rang.

Grace.

"Are you still up?" she asked.

"Yes, are you?" Stupid question. Obviously she was.

"Yes. I'm not sleepy."

"Neither am I. It's all the adrenaline. We've had quite the evening."

"Does wine stop that adrenaline?"

I looked at my still-full glass. "I think so."

"Want to come over?"

"I'll bring the wine. I have some that needs to be drunk soon. It may be close to its expiration date."

"I didn't know wine had an expiration date."

Grace didn't get my sense of humor, but we had formed a bond of sorts.

I got my box of wine from the refrigerator, stuck my phone and stun gun in my pockets, and headed to Grace's. I wouldn't need the stun gun. The bad guy was in jail. But I'd become accustomed to having it with me. One item in each back pocket. Balance.

The evening was chilly, but the rain had stopped. A sliver of moon peeked from behind the clouds. The storm was over. All was calm.

It didn't feel calm. The humid air had a sharp edge.

That wasn't possible. Didn't even make sense.

It was just me.

Adrenaline.

And that ugly truck still parked in front of Grace's house. We would have to get it towed. The Mayfields weren't coming back for it. I wouldn't if it was my truck.

Grace met me at the door with two glasses. "We did it. Time to celebrate."

I put the box of wine on the coffee table. We filled our glasses then sat in the arm chairs. Both of us avoided the sofa.

"I sent Rickie upstairs to bed, but I know he's not asleep," Grace said. "He's so excited about his mother being part of a big drug bust." She sipped her wine. "I didn't tell him we couldn't get that man to admit he killed Chuck."

"He's in custody now. They'll beat it out of him." Interesting that my wine once again tasted okay.

"I don't think they're allowed to beat people."

"No, they're not, but they have ways of getting suspects to confess."

We drank in silence for a few minutes.

"That was lucky George tripped and dropped the box of drugs," she said. "The closer we got to the door, the more worried I got. Do you think he did it on purpose so he wouldn't be caught carrying them?"

I laughed. "Fred tripped him. On purpose."

"Oh." She leaned back in her chair. "That Fred, he's an interesting guy."

"Very."

"He retired from the mob or something?"

I thought of our visit with Donato Orsini. "Maybe."

"You don't know?"

"No."

"Don't you wonder? I mean, he knows a lot of stuff."

"Of course I wonder, but he won't tell me."

"Oh."

I sensed an ally in my ongoing quest to discover Fred's secrets.

We drank in silence again. A comfortable silence.

"I still feel antsy," Grace said. "How much wine does it take to make this adrenaline stop?"

"More than a glass, less than a box."

She got up for a refill then settled back into her chair. My glass was almost empty, but I wasn't going for a refill. I had to go to work in a few hours.

"I'm really sorry about Chuck." I'd said it before and I'd meant it, but tonight my words came from a more personal level. "I know you loved him, and he made you happy."

"He was the love of my life. I used to love Rickie's daddy, but not the same way I loved Chuck."

"I know what you mean. It's hard to love Rickhead."

"I reckon you do know. Rick's like a pretty package wrapped in shiny paper with a big red bow, but when you open it, the box is empty."

Grace might be uneducated, but she wasn't dumb.

"Actually, I think that box might have a little rotten, stinky garbage in it."

Grace giggled. "Week old fish heads."

"Milk you lost in the refrigerator for a month." This was fun, having somebody to trash Rickhead with.

"Rickie's diapers when he was a baby."

"Let me think a minute. That's going to be hard to top."

Someone pounded on the front door.

Chapter Twenty-One

Grace and I sat upright, any banished adrenaline returning in full force.

"You think it's him?" Grace whispered. "Out of jail and come back to get us?"

"I don't know." I took my cell phone and my stun gun out of my pockets. Call Fred? Call Trent? Zap somebody?

Rickie charged down the stairs. "Who's that?"

"Grace, honey, can we come in?" Edwina. Chuck's mother.

Rickie slammed his body against the door. "Go away!"

"It's cold and wet out here," Leon whined.

"Open up!" The screechy voice was vaguely familiar. "You wanted them, you got them!"

Alinn!

Grace shot to her feet, hesitated uncertainly for a moment, then headed for the door.

I went after her. "Don't let them in!"

"No, Mama," Rickie pleaded.

"Your daddy's parents are out there. You let them in right now."

Rickie moved away and allowed his mother to open the door.

Leon and Edwina looked even more bedraggled than they had the night before.

Alinn stood beside them. Anger swirled around her in almost-visible waves. "Take them! They ain't got any money!"

"I know that," Grace said.

Alinn had believed the story about the inheritance for a grandchild, and she was pregnant. She was disgusting and pitiful.

She turned and stomped toward her blue Subaru SUV parked behind the Mayfield's truck.

Rickie pushed between Grace and me, shoved the Mayfields aside, and tackled Alinn in the middle of the yard. Both of them tumbled to the ground.

Grace rushed out behind him. "Rickie! Stop that!"

Stay on the porch with the Mayfields or rush off into battle with Grace and Rickie?

I followed Grace.

Alinn and Rickie struggled in the wet grass. She threw him off and tried to get up, but he held onto her foot.

"Get away from me!" She kicked him.

"You take them back!"

"Let her go," Grace ordered.

Alinn pounded the ground. "I'm gonna sue all of you!"

Grace dragged Rickie away from Alinn. "Why did you stop her? We want rid of her."

"She took them people," Rickie said. "She's got to keep them. We don't want them."

Alinn struggled to her feet and brushed dead leaves off her sweater. Her beady eyes narrowed on Grace, and her scrunchy face scrunched tighter. "This is all your fault! You thought Chuck would adopt that kid and you'd get all the money! Well, there isn't any money, I don't have a husband, and your brat doesn't have a daddy!"

I studied Alinn's angry face, her belligerent stance. She'd known about the adoption. "You believed Chuck's story about his rich parents who wanted a grandchild. You found out he was going to adopt Rickie, give them a grandchild, so you got pregnant. Not by Chuck. He was shooting blanks. But your plan backfired. He's dead, the Mayfields are broke, and you're on your own with a baby on the way."

"She's not pregnant," Rickie said. "I punched her in the gut when we were fighting. There's no baby in there. She's just got a flabby belly."

Alinn's face paled. She spun around and started toward the street.

Grace rushed over and grabbed her arm. "How'd you know about the adoption? He told you, didn't he? He told you he was leaving you for me so you pretended to be pregnant."

Alinn shook off Grace's hand. "Chuck told me everything. I knew about all the women he pretended to marry. We talked about all of you, laughed about how dumb you are."

Grace gasped.

Alinn was going to pay for that remark. "So you want us to believe that you knew all about your husband marrying other women, sleeping with other women? Cheating on you? That didn't bother you?"

She snorted.

The noise was cute when Henry did it. Disgusting when Alinn did it.

"We used all you women! You were nothing but tools."

A couple of puzzle pieces slid into place, but the picture they were creating was surreal.

Howdy Doody's words replayed in my mind. This was all that bitch's idea! She didn't care about Mayfield! She wanted money! I'd thought he was talking about Grace. Now I wasn't so sure. Was it possible this not-very-bright woman could be the one behind the whole wives/churches/drugs thing?

"You knew about all the other women," I said. "You were the first. You helped set up the drug distribution thing."

The woman's squinchy eyes opened so wide they were almost normal sized. "Chuck was my husband. He loved me. That's all."

"You said you used those other women. Dumford wasn't talking about Grace when he said he'd take that bitch down with him. He was talking about you."

That got her attention. "Gaylord? He didn't say that. When? How do you know him?"

"We were there when the cops hauled him away a couple of hours ago. They'll be coming for you soon. Last I saw of him, he was squealing his head off, giving up everybody he knows from the kid who put salt in his Kool-Aid in grade school to the woman he blames for his arrest." I gave her a moment to take that in. "You."

"You're lying." She didn't sound sure.

"You got Chuck into that awful drug business?" Grace lunged toward Alinn but Rickie and I held her. "Let me go! I'll kill that bitch. She killed Chuck!"

"You can't prove that!"

Complete stillness as in a sci-fi movie where the mad scientist stops time.

No dogs barked in the distance. No crickets chirped. No frogs called. No rain fell.

Grace had accused Alinn of killing Chuck by getting him involved in drugs.

Alinn had taken the accusation literally.

She didn't protest her innocence. She simply said we couldn't prove it.

She spun and took a step toward her SUV, toward her escape.

I stuck my foot in her path. I've learned all sorts of useful things from Fred.

She stumbled but regained her balance. "You tripped me!"

"Can't get anything thing past you, can we?"

She blinked. "What?"

"Never mind." I'd stopped her. Now what? What would Fred do? "Dumford told the cops he got the cyanide for you," I lied. More a fishing expedition than a lie. It didn't count against my daily quota.

She charged me, slammed her head into my chest.

I stumbled backward and my stun gun flew out of my hand. I should have followed Fred's advice and put the lanyard around my wrist.

Alinn came after me, but before she made contact again, she screamed, went into a seizure, and fell to the ground.

"Take that, bitch." Rickie brandished my stun gun. "I need one of these."

Grace rushed up and took it away from him.

I reached for it, but she held her hand away, her attention focused on Alinn. "You killed him? You murdered my husband for the money you thought his folks had? Money that doesn't even exist?" Before I could stop her, she zapped Alinn again.

Okay, I didn't try very hard to stop her.

Fred rushed up and grabbed Grace's hand. "That's enough. You don't want to kill her."

Fred?

"She killed my husband! She deserves to die!"

"I know. She'll be punished. Give the stun gun back to Lindsay."

Grace complied but shot Alinn a glare of at least a million volts.

Alinn moaned.

Fred extended a hand to help her up.

She rolled away from him and tried to get up on her own, but her muscles were uncooperative. She flopped around and finally accepted his help.

"Call the police!" she demanded. "These people assaulted me!"

"She started it," I said.

"The police are on their way. I phoned Detective Trent. You were correct, Lindsay. Dumford confessed that he supplied cyanide to this woman. She told him she was going to kill Grace, not Chuck. That was a very astute conclusion."

"I'm becoming psychic like you."

"Get your hands off me!" Alinn shouted.

"I'm sorry, but I can't do that," Fred said. "I witnessed your attacks on Grace and Lindsay. They're afraid for their lives. I am obligated to restrain you until the authorities arrive."

"You're going to be sorry you ever touched me!"

Fred tilted his head away from her. "I already am. How long has it been since you had a bath?"

A police siren screamed down our street.

A squad car pulled over to the curb in front of the ugly truck. Two uniformed officers got out. A familiar dark blue sedan slid into place behind Alinn's vehicle, and Trent got out.

Three officers for one woman?

"Arrest these people!" Alinn struggled but Fred held her effortlessly.

The cops went straight to Alinn. Trent ignored me. Just as well. This wasn't the sort of attention I wanted from him.

One of the uniforms put her in handcuffs while she screamed and cursed.

"You're under arrest for murder," the officer said. She screamed louder. "You have the right to remain silent." That wasn't going to happen. He continued to recite the Miranda warning while she continued to scream.

They put her in the back seat of the squad car. When they closed the door, the night became a great deal quieter.

The squad car drove away.

Trent came over and wrapped his arms around me. "You okay?"

How could anybody be okay after an encounter with that crazy woman? But I wasn't going to admit it. "I'm fine."

"Go home. Try to get some sleep."

"I know. You've got paperwork."

"I'll call you." He gave me a quick kiss then turned and walked away.

Our street was quiet and serene again.

"Everybody all right?" Fred asked.

"I think so," Grace said.

Rickie said nothing.

Fred had done it again. Arrived in the nick of time.

"Where did you come from?" I asked.

"I came from that house across the street and down two. I live there."

"I know that! I mean, what are you doing here? Going for a walk, and you just happened upon us as we were taking Alinn down for murder?"

"I looked out the door when she drove up and saw her herding those people to Grace's front door. Then you all ran out and began shouting so loudly, it was impossible not to hear you."

Those people.

In all the excitement, I'd forgotten about them.

I looked toward Grace's house.

The front door was closed. Television images flickered through the windows. The TV wasn't on when we left.

Rickie followed my gaze and groaned. "How are we going to get rid of them?"

I looked at Grace. The Mayfields were all hers now. Her rival for Chuck's parents was out of the picture. She could have the family she'd wanted. It would be the most dysfunctional family on the planet, but she could have them.

"All you have to do is say the word, and they'll be gone," Fred said.

Say the word! I mentally commanded Grace.

She licked her lips and looked at the truck sitting in the street.

Say the word!

"They were Chuck's parents," she said softly.

Wrong word!

"I'll run away from home and go live with Aunt Lindsay," Rickie said.

Aunt Lindsay?

Grace wrapped an arm around her son. "Get rid of them."

"Wait here." Fred went into Grace's house.

Five minutes later the Mayfields scurried out and, without looking to one side or the other, jumped into their truck.

Fred strolled out behind them and waited with us while they started the truck.

The engine fluttered but finally engaged. Again our street was alive with sound. They rattled away leaving a smelly exhaust trail behind.

Grace choked and fanned the air in front of her face. "Rude people. They didn't even say good-bye."

"What did you tell them?" I asked Fred.

His face was serene in the moonlight as he watched the smoke disappear around the corner. "I simply asked them to leave."

"Thank you!" Grace hugged Fred then me. "If it wasn't for you all, I'd be on my way to prison. I'm so glad we're neighbors!"

I hugged her back. "Me too." What's one little lie between friends?

Grace kissed Rickie's forehead. "It's past your bedtime."

We all said good night. Grace and Rickie walked together up the sidewalk toward their home.

"Can I have a stun gun?" Rickie asked.

Rickie with a stun gun? I waited tensely for Grace's answer.

"No, but we have some of your Aunt Lindsay's cookies left."

Other than the Aunt Lindsay part, it was a good answer.

It was past my bedtime too.

Fred and I crossed the street to my house.

"There's no way you got the Mayfields to leave by simply asking them to go," I said. "What did you really tell them?"

"That the house was rigged with a bomb and would explode in five minutes."

"Really?"

"No."

Maybe having Grace for a neighbor would be a good thing after all. She would be my ally in finding out the truth about Fred.

Chapter Twenty-Two

Friday evening, and all was right with the world.

Trent was in my arms or I was in his. In any event, we were snuggled up on my sofa with an empty pizza box on the coffee table.

Alinn and Dumford were in jail, charged with a lot of drug stuff as well as murder and accessory to murder. They wouldn't be going anywhere for a long time. Laurie Dumford and George were safe.

The Mayfields were gone. Rickie didn't have to run away to live with me.

Henry wouldn't have let that happen anyway.

Trent held me closer. "I worry about you."

"That's sweet but silly. You chase bad guys and put your life in danger. I make chocolate. Other than burning my finger on a hot pan, my job isn't dangerous."

"It's not your job that worries me. It's your extra-curricular activities."

I didn't want to talk about that. "Do you want another beer?" I tried to wriggle away.

He didn't let me go. "No. And before you say it, you don't need another Coke. We need to talk."

Most times I like to talk. This didn't sound like it would be one of those times. I had to divert this train wreck before it happened. We'd already eaten, so I couldn't use chocolate. "I love you."

"I love you too."

"Okay, enough talking. Want to go upstairs?"

"After you tell me why you were avoiding me earlier this week until you got a hair-brained idea to take down a drug dealer and needed my help."

"Have I been avoiding you?" I didn't deny it. I just asked for confirmation.

"Yes."

I didn't like admitting I had been withholding information from him, but it was a relief not to have to keep secrets anymore. "I guess it's okay to tell you now. George found a box of decongestants when he was helping Grace unpack. She didn't want you to know Chuck was involved with that sort of thing, so she made me promise not to tell you."

Trent was either laughing silently or having a seizure. He'd better be having a seizure.

"That was admirable of you to keep Grace's secret," he said, "but I work for the police department. It's our job to know about things like that."

I bristled. "And maybe if you'd tell me what you know, I wouldn't have to keep secrets and I wouldn't have to get involved in those extra-curricular activities! This secrets thing is a two-way street."

"You know I can't tell you what goes on at work."

"Then I can't tell you what goes on in my extra-curricular activities." I wanted to get up, toss my hair, and walk away. But I also wanted to stay right where I was. It had been a long, crazy week. I needed some cuddling.

On the other hand, this was important, something we'd argued about before and never resolved. Well, I'd argued and Trent had gone all stoic and refused to tell me about his work. I tensed and pulled away as much as I could without breaking contact.

He kissed the back of my neck.

"You're not playing fair," I protested.

He kissed my neck again. "I'll answer a question for you, then you answer one for me. Deal?"

I thought about that. "After tonight, I already know everything, so you don't have anything to bargain with."

"How about I tell you the rest of Alinn's confession?"

I did have some unanswered questions about her. "You'd really tell me everything?"

"It's public record. It'll be on the news tomorrow."

"So I could wait until tomorrow and get the information anyway." And then I wouldn't have to answer any of his questions.

"The news may not consider some of the details worthy of inclusion in the story. Your friend, Grace, might be interested in some of those details."

Curiosity struggled with a desire not to confess. Curiosity won. "Okay, I'm listening."

"But you have to tell me about your extra-curricular activities."

"All right, all right, deal."

"Alinn and Dumford go way back. They had a thing going at one time when they were both small-time users and dealers back in Arkansas. But then Dumford moved up here to get away from the law."

"Fred already knew that. Well, not about Alinn."

"Okay," Trent said, "your turn. What do you mean, Fred already knew that?"

"Because when we went to Dumford's house..." Oops. Well, I'd made a deal. My secrets for his. I told him about our visit and how Fred had referred to Dumford's past a couple of times.

He listened silently and didn't laugh this time. I appreciated the not laughing part, but mostly I appreciated the silent part, no reprimands.

Best to end on a positive note. "So Fred helped Laurie escape. Your turn. I want to hear more about Alinn."

"She moved up here with Gaylord, and they continued their association even after he married Laurie. When she met Chuck, he really was only a farm equipment salesman. He wasn't making much money, but he told her that story about his parents being wealthy and estranged and setting up a trust for a grandchild. She didn't get pregnant, of course, and Chuck wasn't making enough money to fund her drug habit. Dumford had a wife and kids, and they were struggling for money too. Alinn and Dumford came up with the drug-to-prison-via-churches idea. They both claim credit for it."

"I'm not sure that's something I would brag about."

"Since Alinn can't boast about her chocolate chips cookies, I guess she has to take her kudos where she can. She and Chuck settled in Leavenworth and got their church connection going while Dumford got his set up. They were so successful, they decided to branch out. Chuck would marry women in other cities and build a network. Alinn didn't care if he slept with other women as long as it he didn't get them pregnant. As we know, that wasn't a problem. Everything was going fine until Grace came along. Chuck told Alinn he was leaving the drugs and Alinn."

"He told Grace the truth. He really did love her."

"So it seems. That was bad enough, but when Alinn found out he was going to adopt Rickie, give his parents a son, and get all that money from the nonexistent gas wells, she got desperate. She faked a pregnancy. With Chuck gone all the time, she didn't think he would figure it out and she could buy a baby when the time came. When he told her the child wasn't his, she decided the only solution was to kill him before he adopted Rickie. Then she could run the baby scam on his parents."

"She told Dumford she wanted the cyanide to kill Grace, so he got it for her. Kill Grace and keep their organization intact." I shivered at the cold brutality of it.

"Alinn persuaded Chuck to come by one last time to tell her good-bye. She dusted his gum with cyanide and hid a package in his suitcase to frame Grace. Then she sat back and waited to hear that he was dead and the woman who almost ruined everything was going to prison."

"Grace needs to know that Chuck loved her and was sort of honest with her. His intentions were honorable. Thank you for telling me that."

"You're welcome. Is there anything else you want to tell me?"

"Not really."

"What about the night you caught George in Grace's house?"

"Oh, yeah, that. I'd kind of forgotten. It wasn't really important in the overall scheme of things. How did you know about that?"

"George told me you called me that night but he convinced you to hang up before I answered. Funniest thing, I don't have any record of an incoming call from you that night."

What a blabbermouth George was! I told Trent the whole story. He laughed about Fred and his shower curtain. He didn't laugh about my stun gun success.

"So everything George did went back to the money he buried in your basement when he and his grandparents lived here."

I flinched. That was a secret I had to keep. "I don't have it."

"I know you don't. But I think you know who does."

My life would be easier if nobody trusted me with their secrets.

I wanted to be honest with Trent. We'd made a deal.

But I'd promised the Murrays I wouldn't tell.

"What makes you think I know anything about it?" When in doubt, equivocate.

"George sent his girlfriend to get that money when he was in prison. At your party, he went after it himself. He thought it was still there. Dumford didn't find it. He was going to kill George if George didn't get it back to him. You didn't find it. You'd never have been able to keep a secret that big. That narrows down the list of suspects."

He knew.

"If you already know, why are you asking me?"

"You're not going to tell me, are you?"

I drew in a deep breath and let it out on a long sigh. "I'm sorry. I can't. I don't want to get some very good people in trouble."

"You do realize you just confirmed what I suspected?"

"That's a relief! I don't have to break my promise to Harold and Cathy!" I clapped a hand over my mouth, but it was too late. Words can't be unsaid.

Trent said nothing.

"I know a lot of people named Harold and Cathy. I serve chocolate to hundreds of people every day, and many of them are named Harold and Cathy."

He continued to say nothing.

"They could be. My customers don't wear name tags."

"I understand. I admire you for keeping your promises. If you make a promise to me, I know you'll keep it."

"Of course."

"Promise me you won't get involved in something dangerous without letting me know first."

I couldn't make a promise I wasn't sure I could keep.

I needed a diversion, one that was more persuasive than the first one I'd tried. I wrapped my arms around his neck and kissed him.

When he drew back, I'd almost forgotten the kiss was supposed to be a diversion.

"Is that a no?" He hadn't forgotten.

"This is silly. I'm not going to get involved in anything dangerous in the future. How about if I promise to think about letting you know before I make the final decision to get involved in anything dangerous should the occasion ever arise?"

He grinned. "I admire your honesty. Do you want to go upstairs?"

I kissed him again.

"Is that a yes?" he asked.

"Definitely a yes."

THE END

(Keep reading for some of Lindsay's favorite recipes!)

RECIPES

Shannon's
Double Chocolate Double Caramel Cake

Cake

1 box devil's food cake mix
Water as specified on mix package
Eggs as specified on mix package PLUS one more
      egg
½ cup butter INSTEAD of oil specified on mix
      package
½ cup unsweetened cocoa
3 tablespoons vanilla

     Stir cocoa into dry mix until evenly distributed. Add water, eggs, butter, and vanilla and mix according to package instructions.

     Grease large rectangular pan (9"x13" or thereabouts) and dust with cocoa. Pour batter into pan and bake according to package instructions.

     Allow cake to cool while still in pan.

Caramel Pudding

6 cups milk
3 eggs
2 cups brown sugar
3/4 cup flour
2 teaspoons vanilla extract
2 tablespoons butter

     Beat together milk and eggs. Add sugar and flour and beat until well mixed. Cook over medium heat until pudding begins to thicken. Remove from heat and add butter and vanilla.

OR

Buy your favorite pudding mix and make according to package directions.

Poke holes in cake with handle of wooden spoon or large straw. If you use the straw, when you're finished, you can suck out all the cake that accumulates in the straw.

Pour warm pudding over cake and allow it to sink into the holes.

Cool cake completely.

<u>Frosting</u>
Carton of Cool-Whip
Jar of caramel sauce

Mix together and frost cake. Sprinkle mini chocolate chips on top.

Chocolate Ganache Cake

<u>Cake</u>
1/2 cup butter, softened
1 cup sugar
4 eggs
1 (16-ounce) can chocolate syrup
1 tablespoon vanilla
1 cup flour

Preheat oven to 325 degrees.

Grease 9 inch bundt pan and dust with cocoa.

Beat butter and sugar until light and fluffy. Add eggs and stir. Add chocolate syrup and vanilla and stir. Add flour and mix until combined. Don't overbeat.

Pour batter into pan. Bake for 40 to 45 minutes or until just set in the middle.

Let cool thoroughly in the pan then turn out onto plate.

<u>Ganache</u>
1/2 cup heavy cream
8 ounces semisweet chocolate chips

Melt chocolate chips and cream in microwave in thirty second increments until chips are dissolved. Allow to cool until it starts to thicken.

Pour ganache evenly over cake. Do not refrigerate.

Ding Dong Cupcakes

<u>Cupcakes</u>
1-1/2 cups flour
1-1/2 cups sugar
3/4 cup cocoa powder
1-1/2 teaspoons baking soda
1 teaspoon baking powder
1/2 teaspoon salt
3/4 cup buttermilk
1/2 cup vegetable oil
2 eggs
1 tablespoon vanilla
3/4 cup warm water

Mix flour, sugar, cocoa, baking soda, baking powder, and salt until evenly combined.

In another bowl, combine buttermilk, oil, eggs, and vanilla.

With the mixer on low speed, slowly add the wet ingredients to the dry. Add water and stir just to combine. Fill 24 cupcake pans half full of batter. Bake for 20 minutes at 350.

Cool completely.

Filling
6 tablespoons flour
1 cup cream
1 tablespoon vanilla
1 cup butter
1 cup granulated sugar

Whisk flour into cream. Cook mixture on medium-low until it thickens. Allow to cool.

Beat butter and sugar until smooth. Add flour mixture and beat a long time until sugar granules are smooth. Add vanilla.

Ganache
2 (12-ounce) packages chocolate chips
1 cup heavy cream
Put in bowl and microwave in two 30 second segments, stirring after each. Continue stirring after second interval until all lumps are gone. Cool.

Put filling on cupcakes. Put ganache on top of filling.

Chocolate Chip Banana Nut Brownies

2 cups flour
1-1/2 cups brown sugar
1/2 cup white sugar
1 cup butter, softened
2 eggs
Dash salt
1 tablespoon vanilla
One banana, mashed
1 (12 ounce) pkg. chocolate chips
1/2 cup chopped nuts

Mix butter, sugars, salt and vanilla with an electric mixer until light and fluffy. Add eggs and mix well.

Add flour and mashed banana and mix well. Add chocolate chips and nuts and stir until combined.

Grease large rectangular pan (9"x13" or thereabouts) and dust with cocoa. Spread mixture into prepared pan.

Bake at 350° for 30-40 minutes until lightly golden brown.

Remove from oven and sprinkle extra chocolate chips on top.

Fred's Favorite Chocolate Cake

<u>Cake</u>
3 cups flour
3 cups sugar
1-1/2 cups unsweetened cocoa powder
1 tablespoon baking soda
1-1/2 teaspoons baking powder
1 teaspoon salt
4 eggs
1-1/2 cups buttermilk
1-1/2 cups warm water
1/2 cup vegetable oil
1 tablespoon vanilla

Preheat oven to 350 degrees.

Grease large rectangular pan (9"x13" or thereabouts) and dust with cocoa.

Mix together flour, sugar, cocoa, baking soda, baking powder, and salt.

Add eggs, buttermilk, warm water, oil, and vanilla. Beat on medium speed until smooth. Do not overbeat.

Pour batter into pan. Bake for 30-35 minutes until toothpick comes out clean.

Chocolate Cream Cheese Frosting

1 cup butter, softened
8 oz cream cheese, softened
1 cup unsweetened cocoa powder
1 tablespoon vanilla extract
5-6 cups powdered sugar
about ¼ cup milk (as needed)

Beat together butter and cream cheese until fluffy.

Add cocoa powder and vanilla extract. Beat until combined.

Beat in powdered sugar, 1 cup at a time. Add milk as necessary to make a spreadable consistency.

Back by popular demand:
Lindsay's Not-So-Secret Chocolate Chip Cookies
1/2 c. butter, softened

1-1/2 c. dark brown sugar

1 egg

1 Tbsp. vanilla

1/2 tsp. baking soda

dash of salt (bigger dash if you use unsalted butter)

1-1/2 c. flour

1/4 c. oat flour (put oats in blender if you don't have
    this on hand)

1/4 c. hazelnut meal (optional but suggested)

1 cup semi-sweet chocolate chips

1 cup bittersweet chips

1/4 cup white chocolate chips

1/2 c. chopped nuts, unless someone is allergic

Cream butter with sugar until light and fluffy. Add egg and vanilla and stir briskly until well mixed. Combine dry ingredients and add to butter mixture. Stir in chocolate chips and nuts. Dough should be very stiff and just a little sticky.

Form dough into balls (I use an ice cream scoop to measure dough) and lay on cookie sheet. Bake at 375° for 7-8 minutes, depending on size of cookie and whether you have a regular oven or convection.

*Hazelnut meal can be difficult to find. I order Bob's Red Mill online.

It can be omitted or almond meal can be substituted.

Without hazelnut or almond meal: "These cookies are
    wonderful!"

With almond meal: "These cookies are amazing!"

With hazelnut meal: "OMG! These are the best cookies
    I've ever eaten!"

About the Author:

I grew up in a small rural town in southeastern Oklahoma where our favorite entertainment on summer evenings was to sit outside under the stars and tell stories. When I went to bed at night, instead of a lullaby, I got a story. That could be due to the fact that everybody in my family has a singing voice like a bullfrog with laryngitis, but they sure could tell stories—ghost stories, funny stories, happy stories, scary stories.

For as long as I can remember I've been a storyteller. Thank goodness for computers so I can write down my stories. It's hard to make listeners sit still for the length of a book! Like my family's tales, my stories are funny, scary, dramatic, romantic, paranormal, magic.

Besides writing, my interests are reading, eating chocolate and riding my Harley.

Contact information is available on my website. I love to talk to readers! And writers. And riders. And computer programmers. Okay, I just plain love to talk!

http://www.sallyberneathy.com

Made in the USA
Middletown, DE
23 April 2022